I0847001

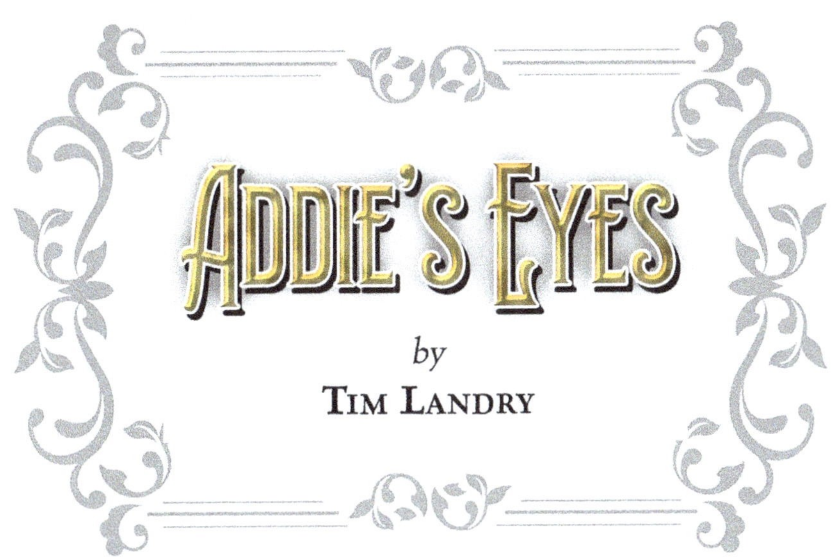

ADDIE'S EYES

by

TIM LANDRY

ILLUSTRATIONS

by

NATALIIA KRETSU

Paperback Edition

ISBN: **979-8-89778-595-7**

For more info on the web, visit:
http://AddiesEyes.com

First Edition Autumn 2025 by Sir Reel Press, a division of Sir Reel Pictures

28200 Pimlico Way, Tehachapi California 93561

http://www.TimLandry.com

To Mauriène, my wife, partner and inspiration.

Foreword

BY

JERRY REES

The first thing you should know about Tim Landry is that millions of people like you – and very likely you yourself – have already taken emotionally profound adventures inside of his imaginative mind.

And by inside, I mean immersed in dynamically themed architecture while riding among audio-animatronic figures, inter-active projections, dimensional audio, and reach-out-and-touch-you effects.

His mischievous pixie dust lured you through the magic storms of Hong Kong Disneyland's *Mystic Manor*. His enchanted paints and storytelling shadows reawakened the spirits of Camellia Falco and her falcon muse Aletta to lift you toward your loftiest dreams in Tokyo DisneySeas' *Soaring: Fantastic Flight*. And when your heart needed reassurance that love would indeed conquer all, Tim's epic and tender visual effects artistry in Disneyland Paris' *Cinemagique* took you by the hand and guided you through the adventures, romances, heartbreaks, and triumphs of a century of cinema before delivering the primal hug you'd been longing for, and a final sweet skip along the yellow brick road toward the Emerald City. For the first time, Oz felt like going home.

I know Tim's imagination intimately. In my role as media Director for all of the above Disney Theme Park Attractions, I knew that Tim would surpass every expectation for excellence and genuine emotion to create indelible memories for our guests.

Tim's natural ability to embody Disney Magic in a deeply authentic way – fully innovative while avoiding superficial novelty, and sincerely grounded in mind and heart – had drawn me to him from the moment we met. His perspective resonated with my roots as a Disney Feature Animator, mentored by Walt Disney's veteran animators – his legendary "Nine Old Men". They experienced Walt as an inspirational man from Kansas, an incessant inventor, a teller of consequential stories, and a guy who'd invite you over for a ride on miniature railroads in his back yard, not as a brand. They told me never to forget it.

I draw a dividing line through the Walt Disney Company. On one side are those who perceive the name of Walt Disney as a corporate logo. On the other side are those who remain keenly aware of the squiggly, hand-inked signature behind the polished logo that belonged to a flawed genius who collected a family of treasured individuals around him – people who inspired him as much as he inspired them, and increased the collective odds of achieving big dreams. Tim is on this side of the line. He is the sort of individual whom Walt would have treasured and added to his family of dreamers.

So, when Tim contacted me with the humble request that I consider reading his manuscript of *Addie's Eyes,* I not only agreed to read it, the prospect of diving into his vivid imagination once again filled me with an excitement equivalent to being handed a booklet filled with Disneyland E tickets back in 1970. I knew I was in for a magical ride.

As usual, Tim exceeded my expectations.

I read *Addie's Eyes* aloud to my wife Rebecca. She too has deep artistic roots as a Disney Feature Animator, and an unquenchable love for reading – a love recently disrupted as the sudden onset of Parkinson's robbed her of the ability to hold a book. But now she didn't have to hold the book, or even try to focus her tired eyes on the page. She could just close her eyes and listen as the story unfolded effortlessly and poetically in her mind – composed by Tim, spoken by me, and seen through *Addie's Eyes.*

Over a series of evenings, Addie spoke through me. Fedor spoke through me. Brother and Toybox and Rachel and many more unforgettable characters spoke through me, as my wife and I shared their wildly unpredictable and emotionally riveting journey.

Somehow, in moving from the boisterous 4-dimensional playground of theme parks to the singular focus of crafting words on a page, Tim's imagination grew. And his storytelling voice grew in originality as well – channeling the unique language of a new world to rival Neverland, Wonderland and the Hundred Acre Wood. I'm grateful that Tim has added a new zip code to my precious map of literary sanctuaries.

I must tell you that at times the story so moved me that reading aloud had to wait for a tear to find its way down my cheek, and for my voice to find enough bravery to come back out of hiding. Tears don't take sides – grief and joy conjure them equally, and Tim conducts both with care.

There was a sense of healing in the story – beyond a glimmer of hope that injured souls and broken systems might be repaired. Tim's cleverness at metaphorical solution-building leapt off the page for me in ways that made key passages seem instantly time-less and iconic in the manner of Lewis Carroll, A. A. Milne, Roald Dahl, or C. S. Lewis. "People will refer to this scene from now on," I'd think. And the world would be better off if they did. We need stories like this now.

In my heart, I'm certain that *Addie's Eyes* is a tale that Walt Disney himself would embrace if he were still with us.

What I treasure most is that Tim made me care deeply about every one of his charming characters all the way to the very last word of the very last sentence on the very last page. And I'm not kidding. (No cheating, you must take each magical step to earn that final moment!) Tim found every opportunity to keep me guessing, so that each bit of discovery – from unveiling epic realms to intimate revelations of plot and character – sparkled.

Fearlessly heartfelt and original, Tim invites us into a world where love, understanding, reconciliation, and sometimes survival itself, seem impossible until we dare to see it all through *Addie's Eyes.*

And you will soon discover what a miracle that is.

Rebecca and I loved it. You will too.

And if you're anything like us, as soon as you're finished reading, you'll ask Tim, "So, when can we expect your next book?!"

— Jerry Rees

Mr. Rees is an Animator, Film Director, Artist, and Imagineer. He is a major creative voice who has brought us some of the best in award-winning themed entertainment. He is probably best known as the director of the classic animated feature **The Brave Little Toaster.**

Prologue

A small tender boat slipped through tranquil Aegean waters bound for the *SS Sirius*, a steamer anchored in the bay just outside the Grecian port of Saloniki. The sun neared the horizon in the waning hours of December 27, 1903. The small craft's sole cargo was one Joseph Rutherford, a thin man of forty with angled features and a hastily trimmed beard. He was being ferried to the larger ship from docks not far away. His dress was dignified but not necessarily tidy, a formula one might expect of a writer. As Rutherford casually observed the white rocks, parched cliffs, and cerulean tones of the water, he tried to imagine what another writer, the Apostle Paul, must have thought when he first arrived on these shores so many centuries ago.

The *Sirius* herself would move into the harbor in the morning when her berth would become available and commence the unloading of her passengers and cargo. Until then, she slept peacefully in the lavender and amber tones of the on-coming

Mediterranean sunset, with only the occasional call from an exotic bird coming from on board the ship or the high-pitched whinny of a zebra to pierce the calm. As is common with winters in the Aegean, the air was crisp but not cold. Rutherford raised his collar for more comfort against the sea air, slung the strap of his leather valise over his shoulder, and put his hands in his pockets as his craft neared the ship. There were lights burning, but scant little activity was evident aboard the *Sirius*.

When a deck hand lowered a rope ladder over the side of the ship, Rutherford's pulse quickened slightly as he anticipated the rendezvous that awaited him. It would be an interview that he had long sought, hoping that it would lead not only to a promotion and personal recognition but perhaps to more choice assignments in the future. For now, the calm of this evening seemed a perfect setting for an intimate interview.

As the small boat got closer, the uniformed purser aboard the *Sirius* called out a Greek phrase in their direction that Rutherford knew none of. But the pilot of the tender boat translated for him, "Identify yourself."

"Joseph Rutherford, *Times of London*," Rutherford shouted. The purser checked his manifest and, after a few tense seconds, waved him ahead. The tender pilot nudged the boat closer to the hull of the ship so that Rutherford was able to gain a firm grasp on the rope ladder and pull himself up and aboard. As his feet hit the deck, the uniformed purser offered his hand. "You are English, Mr. Rutherford?" he managed with a heavy accent. Rutherford shook the hand he'd been offered.

"Yes, sir. I'm a reporter with the *Times of London*. I'm told that you have a special passenger in stateroom five?"

"Yes, sir. He is expecting you. Right this way, please." Rutherford followed his mustachioed host forward. Along their way, he noticed that this was a fairly well-kept ship. There was a smell of fresh paint, and things were generally in good repair, which was more than he could say for the previous vessel he'd been on. Every spare inch of the deck—and presumably below decks as well—was filled with a vast variety of sturdy wooden crates, each painted in a bright rainbow colour but exhibiting many miles of wear. Some of the crates were stenciled "Menagerie" on their outside and had small barred windows in them. Shadows of exotic creatures could occasionally be glimpsed through those windows, and the cries of animals erupted as Rutherford and the purser passed by.

Rutherford reflected on his good fortune in landing this assignment. He didn't often get celebrity interviews. When Collins, his editor, had handed it to him, he relished not only the prime assignment but the opportunity to discover more about his subject—a man who was known worldwide and yet had remained distinctly obscure.

Shortly, the two men passed a sign on a bulkhead proclaiming "First Class: Staterooms 1 - 8." A moment later, they found themselves at the cabin door of stateroom five.

"You have one hour, Mr. Rutherford. The tender boat will return at that time to take you back to shore."

Rutherford grimaced a little. An hour didn't seem like much after all this. But he was gracious. "That will be fine, mister…?"

"Pekkanen. Please let us know if there is anything that you need."

"Thank you, mister Pekkanen." With that, the purser stepped away and left Rutherford to his task.

Rutherford paused. Interviews had sometimes been challenging for him. But he vowed to be at the peak of his abilities with this one. He took a deep breath and knocked.

"You may enter," came the salutation from within.

Gingerly opening the door, Rutherford, not knowing exactly what to expect, found himself in a nicely appointed suite with a small chandelier, leather wingback chairs, and its own wet bar. A large, gilt-framed circus poster on one wall boldly proclaimed "Jo-Jo the Dog-Faced Boy." Two substantial bookcases, filled with leather-bound volumes, adorned the other walls.

"Mr. Rutherford?" a gentle voice asked from one of the wing-back chairs. And then Rutherford realized—there he *was*! A man of perhaps thirty in a satin robe with leather slippers occupied the chair. His entire face and hands were obscured with long, soft brown and grayish hair, nicely combed. "Jo-Jo!" he exclaimed, "What a delight it is to finally meet you." After a brief breath to regain himself, he shook the younger man's hand.

"You can call me Fedor," said the young man. "Jo-Jo is my character name. Uh…Forgive me for not getting up just now. I'm feeling a bit tired." He coughed briefly and reached for a silver dish laden with red and orange candies, passing it toward Rutherford. "May I offer you a gumdrop?" Rutherford detected only a slight Russian accent in his voice.

"That's quite all right, Fedor. And by the way, my name is Joseph, and you may call me Joe if you wish."

A wry smile came across Fedor's lips. "If you had a Siamese twin brother, Joe, perhaps *you* could be Joe-Joe!" he chuckled. Rutherford appreciated that Fedor was trying to put him at ease and, when he smiled broadly, Fedor continued. "Very well then, Joe. How may I best be of service to you?" Rutherford observed that on one side of Fedor's chair was a small round table stacked with half a dozen books consisting of classics and poetry. Each had a bookmark partway through it. The other side of the chair had a similar small table stacked with the latest newspapers. The paper on top, Rutherford noted, was turned and folded to display one of his own pieces.

"You've come at a good time," explained Fedor. "Saloniki is our last stop on this tour. The show opens tomorrow night." He adjusted himself in the chair and took a deep breath. "I can get you tickets if you'd like."

Rutherford drew up the other leather chair. "I would like that very much," he offered, noting Fedor's apparent discomfort. "You…you've already done a lot just by agreeing to speak with me today, sir. But if I may…why now? Why me? The press has been wanting to speak with you for years. And yet, your bosses have always shooed us away. They only want us to tell your story as *they* feed it to us."

"You have to understand, Mr. Ruther—Joe, that the business that employs me and those like me thrives and exists on fantasy and the exotic. We understand that the public wants something fanciful. And, in striving to provide what the customers want, fantastic tales are manufactured to embellish what the customer's own eyes are actually seeing. My employers don't want to break the spell. It's bad for business, they say. But despite all that, I've begun to feel that my real story might actually be more stimulating to the imagination than anything the carny touts could ever come up with."

"But again, why me?" Rutherford grabbed his valise and took out his notepad and pencil.

"I've read your work, Joe." Fedor held up *The Times*. "It feels honest. It feels thorough. And most of all, it feels human."

"I'm very flattered, sir. But I can only write what I see and hear. So help me to write something honest and human—where does your story begin?"

Fedor leaned a bit toward Rutherford and took a breath.

"They call me the dog-faced boy. I have a condition the doctors call hypertrichosis. I simply grow more hair than most people. It's been this way all my life, so I've never known anything different. I used to feel God had cursed me for something I or my parents must have done. But gradually I've come to understand that it isn't a curse. God has used my condition as a way to providentially provide for me, a way I can make a living."

Rutherford nodded. "Yes, I understand you're one of the most successful and well-paid personalities in the business. Uh… what exactly would you call your business, sir?"

"Some call it the sideshow. Or the freak show. Others just call us human curiosities. People tend to look on myself and my colleagues with pity, or curiosity, or horror. We engender strong emotions. And those strong emotions are what allow my friends and myself to survive when many of us would otherwise find ourselves destitute."

"Where were you born, Fedor?" queried Rutherford, his head down, scribing frantically.

"That's a little hard to say. You see, I never knew my father. And my mother's eyesight was so poor that they took me away from her when I was three. But I'm told I come from the region of St. Petersburg in Russia. The people I ended up with, like most in that land, were very poor. When they discovered my condition, they quickly realized I had a certain kind of value. They sold me to a traveling fair…"

Rutherford looked up, "*Sold* you?"

"I don't know how else one would put it. Things are not the same in rural Russia as they are in London, Joe. At the age of three, I joined the ranks of animals, acrobats, and dancers. Show business of some form became the only way of life I knew. It didn't have any sort of glamour, though. It was simply my life."

Fedor sighed as he revisited those fragmented early memories: leering faces, splashes of colour, shouts of show barkers, the smells of frying food, and the cries of unhappy animals.

"The guardians I had over me were sometimes kind and caring toward a child who didn't understand what was happening to him. They taught me manners and how to speak and even to read. Other guardians were more cruel, treating me as one of the show's animals. For long periods, I was kept in a cage and was harshly disciplined when I disobeyed, and often even when I didn't."

Fedor stared off into space for a moment as the harsh clanging of cages, the bitter Russian cold, and the noxious smells came rushing back to him from all those years ago.

"Do you remember your mother?" asked Rutherford.

Fedor was glad to be dragged back to the present and paused as he processed Rutherford's question. "I have only impressions of her holding me close. It was the only way she could show me affection. Her voice was very tender, I recall."

"Was she…like you?"

"Did she have extra hair? I don't remember for myself. Some have said that she did, others that she didn't. I simply don't remember." Fedor strained to recall more of his mother, realizing his memories were perhaps coloured more by his longing for the loving care she briefly afforded him than they were by actuality.

Rutherford changed the subject, "What kind of performances did you do in those early days?"

"There was a man from a village near mine in Russia who also had hypertrichosis. His name was Adrian Evtikheev. He had met an entrepreneur named Foerster, who convinced Adrian to tour with me as if we were father and son…We became the 'Wild People of Kostroma.' The barkers told a tale to the people that we had been discovered in a cave by Russian hunters deep in the forest and lived on wild berries and such. Adrian and I had little to do in the show but sit there as the barkers told our story, a story that seemed to change nightly and got wilder and stranger as time went on. We toured a number of Russian fairs with Mr. Foerster, and we were so popular that the fairs came to depend on our appearances for their own survival. So we were able to make substantial demands for our services and ended up being well paid. But since, at the time, both Adrian and myself considered our ugliness to be God's punishment, we gave much of our earnings to the poor and to monasteries. I was only five, so I don't remember a whole lot of this. After a break from the Russian cities tour, we continued on for several years to tour all of Europe. But success did not do well by Adrian. He refused to eat anything other than his beloved sauerkraut and vodka because…well, I suppose because he could. After the Europe tour, he was homesick and returned to Russia, the homeland of his cherished vodka. He loved it so much that he soon died of alcoholism there."

Rutherford grimaced. "So then you were on your own…a solo act?"

"After Adrian's passing, not quite knowing what to do with me, the fairs at first just kept me in a cage in the sideshow tent. The people would walk past, stare at me for a moment, and keep walking. Later on, my employers coaxed me to growl and bark, even made me chew on pieces of raw meat. All this seemed to please the customers tremendously, and my manager started to pay me more as I got older and the show receipts grew. But I still felt it was undignified." Fedor paused. "Touring for those years meant I grew up on the road. I got to visit many places I never would otherwise have seen and meet a lot of people, both show people and others. I learned several languages, including English, by the way."

Rutherford offered, "Yes, your English is marvelous."

"As is yours," Fedor smiled and winked. "I have no regrets from those days, even though the touring was difficult. But one day in early 1882, I met a man named Charles Reynolds who said he wanted to manage me, get me into better venues, and make more money. I was still just twelve, but his pitch made it sound like life would be a bit easier, so I signed with him.

"Charlie made good on his promise," Fedor continued. "The types of shows and the quality of life improved for both him and me. But it wasn't perfect. Touring was still touring, and Charlie, too, had a penchant for the bottle."

"You also worked for P.T. Barnum, correct?" asked Rutherford.

"I toured America and Australia with him and his circus for several years. It was Mr. Barnum himself who came up with the name 'Jo-Jo the Dog-Faced Boy.' He was such the consummate showman that I couldn't really argue. His original show story for me was that I'd been raised by wolves in the forests of Russia. The crowds really responded to that idea. In all the other shows I had worked, I was usually in a booth inside the sideshow tent. And it was the same at first with Barnum. But as the crowds grew, Barnum realized we could do more. He moved me into the main show under the Big Top. They created an elaborate and beautiful pageant that depicted me being presented to the tsar of Russia. It was very impressive; the crowds loved it. And for me, the best part of the Barnum tour was that as a part of a circus, I was able to interact with many more children, which I adored."

"So you have no children of your own? I take it you are not married," queried Rutherford.

"I was almost married!" Fedor smiled. "Several years ago, a promoter broadly announced my engagement to a hypertrichotic girl from Michigan they called Kee-Boo. She was nice enough, very quiet. We only met once or twice, I think. The wedding was to take place in New York. But it was really all for the ballyhoo, and it finally never happened. I'm not even sure why."

"There's been no one for you then? Have you ever fallen in love?" Rutherford braved getting more personal.

Fedor got quiet. He leaned back in his chair and stared off across the room once more. Rutherford feared he had crossed a line. "Fedor, I'm sorry if I'm getting too private, I just…"

"It's quite all right, Joe." He offered with a slight smile. "I was just remembering. There was once a special young lady who captured my heart. We were not lovers as you might imagine it. And we barely even got to know each other." He paused, his voice getting softer. "But we were definitely soul mates…"

RUBY PALACE THEATRE

Chapter One
NINETEEN YEARS EARLIER

On a June afternoon in 1884, Liverpool's Ruby Palace Theatre building was fairly quiet before the mad rush to make ready for the evening's performance. Twelve-year-old Addie Alexander was perched on a settee in the lobby of her father's theatre, folding a piece of paper in very deliberate fashion. She wore an everyday grey dress with ruffled sleeves and a lace collar, and her ashen blonde hair was tied in braids. But before she finished her paper-folding task, a thought occurred. She reached into the pocket of her skirt and found a penny, which she walked across the lobby to feed into the slot of the massive band organ that filled one wall. Her father had imported this device from America in his efforts to add more value for the theatre's patrons. The mechanical marvel contained almost every imaginable type of instrument. With violin, piano, xylophone, and tambourine, the mechanized behemoth began churning forth a quaint medley of Stephen Foster tunes that would ultimately culminate with Addie's favourite, "Beautiful

Dreamer." Addie smiled. The silence was more than broken. The music, boisterous and tinny as it was, made her happy.

Liverpool, in the summer of 1884, was a bustling and raucous port town, reeling from the rapid growth of a railroad and the cotton trade. Additionally, it had become the second-largest seaport in the British Empire. Immigrants of many flavors poured in from all over Europe and the world. A quarter of Liverpool's populace hailed from Ireland, and there were substantial communities of immigrants from Wales, Africa, and China.

These were mostly working people who had to be housed, fed, and, due to their increasingly steady wages, entertained. This need for entertainment often took the form of live theatrical offerings. There were several theatres of various sizes in Liverpool. Their working-class clientele tended to be somewhat loud and rowdy in 1884.

But it had been worse in previous decades. In 1862, The Liverpool *Porcupine* newspaper printed the following:

"We have in Liverpool four theatres and a circus, wretched buildings...a disgrace to us and totally unsuited to the purposes for which they are used.

What can be worse than the locales of the Theatre Royal and the Royal Amphitheatre? Every sense is offended as the visitor approaches them. The stenches from market refuse and close, dank, reeking streets are even dangerous to health, while the sights and sounds are so offensive that hundreds of ladies are denied the pleasure of theatrical entertainments.

At the Theatre Royal, the chairs in the dress circle are hard and far too small, and the sitting room in other parts of the house as beggarless and comfortless as possible. At the Amphitheatre, matters are even worse. The ventilation is wretched, in summer the ardent playgoer is parboiled, while in winter the icy air from both stage and lobbies is enough to freeze even a polar bear.

Behind the curtain, matters are even worse. The stages above and below are encumbered with useless antiquated machinery: the dressing rooms are the veriest dog-holes, while the whole place – dangerous from absence of light is pervaded by noisome smells. That the musicians whose wretched fate it is to sit in the orchestras are ever free from colds and rheumatism speaks wonders for the acclimatizing powers of human nature."

By the 1880s, when the burgeoning town officially became a city, and more than twenty years since the above publication, there were ongoing efforts to improve the standing of Liverpool's theatrical offerings. Part of this upward movement was sustained by one Ezra Alexander, a clean-shaven, dark-haired widower in his late thirties who determined to devote his recently acquired inheritance to the creation of a new theatre for the presentation of "lively entertainments for all guests to enjoy, not excluding ladies and children." Mr. Alexander took on this enterprise as a tribute to his lovely and talented late wife Annabelle, a stunning beauty from Vienna who had dearly loved the theatre arts both as a performer and a patron. He vowed to keep her memory alive in the form of a new home for the arts.

The project took the form of the acquisition and renovation

of an existing stone building in the Clayton Square area on London Road. It would not be the largest venue in Liverpool, Ezra's designs being modest, but it would cast its eye toward quality of presentation that could be sustained and built upon for the long term. The original building had been a combination warehouse and office building, and Ezra acquired it at a good price from the family of its deceased owner. With its existing offices and rooms spread over four stories and a basement, along with a rear warehouse space that could easily become a stage and auditorium, the conversion to a theatre would be accomplished largely by the mere addition of Classical and Rococo adornments to the frontal facade.

In addition, there was a hotel only steps away that could accommodate traveling performers, along with multiple pubs and eating establishments along the adjoining streets that would not only feed but supply customers to the theatre. And, not the least of the appeals of the property was the fact that it was but walking distance from the residential street that harbored a Queen-Anne style house that Ezra Alexander and his daughter Addie called home.

So it happened in the spring of 1879 that the former office building officially re-opened with as much fanfare as Ezra and his team could muster as The Ruby Palace Theatre. Its early entertainment offerings consisted of singers, orators, comics, dancers, jugglers, and acrobats, among others. It was diverting enough to keep the populace satisfied, and Ezra's theatre enterprise soon flourished. This was quite an accomplishment for a playhouse that contained a mere eight hundred and fifty seats.

After bringing the Band Organ to life, Addie returned to her seat to continue her paper-folding effort. She located the piece, ran her fingers around the edges to take stock of its progress, and continued folding. It was Saturday and her schoolwork for the week was complete, allowing her to spend time in her father's theatre with all its bustle, music, and novel personalities. Within a couple of minutes, she finished her paper project—an origami turtle. Shortly thereafter, the churning music organ finished its presentation and, following a moment of whispered mechanical chugging, shut itself off. Silence reigned once more.

At that moment, fifty-six-year-old Walter Hodge, the theatre's long-time silver-haired caretaker, began his pass through the lobby pushing his dry mop. He muttered to himself about the band organ. "Ooh, thank goodness. That old noisy thing. Now, maybe I can do my cleaning in peace." On spotting Addie, he smiled. "Why, good day, Miss Addie. How's every little thing with you today?"

"Hello, Mr. Hodge," she brightened, standing to meet him. "I made you something."

"You made a present for me, young lady?"

"Uh-huh. Hold out your hand."

Walter leaned his mop against a chair back and dutifully complied. In his hand, Addie gingerly placed the origami turtle she had just completed.

A big smile grew on Walter's face. "Why, it's a turtle! How did you do that?"

"Rachel taught me," Addie boasted. "Actually, it's a terrapin, but you can call it a turtle."

Suddenly, just outside, a dog began barking frantically. A woman screamed and then could be heard shouting, "Nigel! Get away from him this instant!" Walter peered out the beveled glass windows of the theatre's front doors to witness the debarkation of two figures from a carriage. One, a balding man in his late fifties with greying sideburns and dark, bushy eyebrows, clutched one end of a rope that was attached to a leather collar around the neck of the other figure, less than five feet tall, who was robed in a dark greyed-purple hooded cloak, the face not visible to Walter. The balding man retrieved his bowler from the carriage and handed some coins to the driver.

"What is it, Mr. Hodge?" Addie asked.

"I think a couple of our performers just arrived," he said, continuing to watch out the window. A couple of boys, six and seven, continued following the pair, throwing pebbles and small sticks at the hooded figure. Finally, having had enough, the balding man got his partner's attention and then subtly but sharply nodded his head toward the children. The hooded figure knew what to do and immediately let out a threatening growl, lunging toward the insistent urchins. This precipitated more screams, tears, and terrified children retreating down the street as the mysterious duo turned to make their way up the alley toward the stage entrance.

Walter chuckled. "That taught 'em," he muttered.

"What happened?" asked Addie.

"Never mind, Honey. We shall meet them soon enough, I expect." He picked up his mop and resumed his daily task.

No sooner had Walter pushed his mop onward into the corridor than a pair of creaky shoes entered the lobby from the rear, where the stage entrance had admitted their owner and his hooded companion. The balding man carried a satchel in one of his gloved hands, his bowler and the end of his charge's rope in the other. The satchel was emblazoned with white text proclaiming: "Charles Reynolds presents the Dog-Faced Boy." He wore a dark brown tailcoat, his features weary from traveling. Reynolds paused a moment, taking in his surroundings, including Addie, who seemingly paid him no notice as she resumed her paper folding.

He lowered the satchel, thereby freeing his hand to attract her attention with a flourishing bow. "Excuse me, sweetheart…"

Addie turned toward him, "Yes?" Yet their eyes did not meet, which, judging by the awkward pause, revealed to her that the visitor had been taken off guard; it had suddenly become evident to him that Addie was blind.

"Er…ah…Where might I find the management of this fair establishment?" Reynolds recovered, stammering.

"Papa's office is upstairs in the back," she replied with a proud smile, gesturing in the direction. She loved the fact that her father reigned as the sovereign of this magical world. Addie's friendly smile did not go unnoticed by the pair of vaguely canine brown eyes peering out from the shadowing hood of Reynolds' companion.

"Thank you," Reynolds offered as he picked up his satchel and turned back down the corridor toward the stairs. But in so doing, he had to give the rope a slight tug to encourage his companion to follow him.

Ezra Alexander was in his cluttered office, collar unbuttoned, tallying figures at his desk. It was that unavoidable day of the week when the theatre's books needed to be balanced. A knock at the door attempted to disturb him, but Ezra didn't look up. "What is it?" he barked.

The door opened to reveal Reynolds, who stood silently until Ezra finally glanced up to discover him. Ezra broke into a grin and chuckled, "Charlie? Charlie Reynolds! You old theatre rat!" He stepped around the desk to give Reynolds a back-slapping handshake. "My god, how long has it been?"

Reynolds was equally surprised to encounter his old colleague. "Ezra, my boy! This is *your* place?! I knew there was nothing that could keep the grease paint out of your blood."

"Whatever brings you around here, Charlie?" Ezra inquired. Reynolds held up his satchel marquee.

"Well, I'll be!" exclaimed Ezra. "The booking agent never told me it was *you*! Come in! Come in!" Reynolds stepped further into the office, followed by his hooded companion, who emerged from the corridor.

"So this must be…?" Ezra paused.

"That's right," Reynolds boasted. "The amazing Dog-Faced Boy, discovered by hunters in the darkest, most remote reaches of the great Kostroma forest in tsarist Russia! Come on in, boy."

The hooded boy complied, shuffling into the small office, his head down.

"Well then…let's have a look," sought Ezra.

"Uh, certainly, seeing as how you're a paying customer…" Reynolds blustered, tugging on the rope. "Step into the light, boy. It's all right." As the fourteen-year-old hirsute boy stepped forward, Reynolds slowly lowered the hood that kept his face obscured.

Ezra's eyebrows went up. "Extraordinary! Is…is this real, all this hair?"

"One hundred percent genuine, Ezra. You can tug on it if you desire," he boasted. Fedor stood silent, his eyes cast downward, wincing at the thought of someone else pulling at his hair. The hair across his face was neatly combed, parting in the centre and generally flowing outward and down. Even his eyelids exhibited the soft, brownish colour hair he had been born with. Some had said he had the appearance of a Skye terrier, hence the "dog-face" moniker.

"You've really got something here, Charlie. If your act is as good as they say, we're going to have a great run," noted Ezra. "Uh, how did you come to…?"

"Purely by accident, really," Reynolds began, taking a breath to launch into his well-oiled patter. Then he paused. He had been doing this for years and was beginning to weary of delivering the same spiel over and over, even to an old friend such as Ezra. "But you know, Ezra, my boy, that's a story that's best told as part of our performance," he stated frankly as he replaced the hood over the boy's head.

"All right, all right," conceded Ezra, waving his hand. "You're on at eight-fifteen, right after the Irish Nightingale."

Reynolds grinned, "Ah, it's great to be together again after these many years, Ezra. Do you remember when we cut holes in the pockets of that magician's jacket?" Both men chuckled.

"Yeah, we had doves and rabbits all over the theater," reminisced Ezra, smiling.

"I must say I'm a bit surprised to see you back on the boards after Annabelle broke up the act and stole you away. Speaking of Annabelle, where is she?" Charlie queried.

"Uh…She's dead, Charlie—when Addie was born," Ezra said matter-of-factly.

Reynolds was shocked. "Oh, I am sorry, Ezra. She was… uh…Addie?"

"Our daughter."

At that moment Addie appeared at the office door, light bamboo cane in one hand and her latest origami creation in the other. "Papa, I have something to…Oh, you have company." She halted abruptly, wrinkling her nose slightly.

Ezra realized she had smelled the liquor on Reynolds' breath, "Uh, Addie, come in. I'd like you to meet a very *old* friend of mine…"

"But young of heart," Reynolds raised a finger and added with a smile. "Reynolds is the name, my dear. Charlie Reynolds." He extended his hand to shake, which, of course, Addie did not see.

"I'm very pleased to meet you, Mr. Reynolds," she replied, curtsying.

Embarrassed, Reynolds withdrew his hand. "Likewise, I'm sure, Miss Adelaide."

"Just Addie, thanks," she replied pragmatically.

Reynolds turned to Ezra, "Lovely girl, Ezra. Reminds me of her mother…only more so." He chuckled nervously.

Addie cocked her head slightly as she heard this, not really understanding what he had said, but knowing she didn't quite trust Reynolds.

Fedor, the Dog-Boy, took all this in silently but intently. His role was to remain mute when in the presence of outsiders. But he found he couldn't keep his eyes off of Addie. Somehow, he felt he already knew her—from another town, or a song, or a dream. It was a feeling that perplexed him.

Ezra addressed Addie, "Sweetheart, these gentlemen are going to be with us for…four days, Charlie?"

"That's correct. Six performances, including matinees," confirmed Reynolds.

"Gentlemen?" asked Addie.

"Uh, yes, dear. This is my partner. He doesn't speak," Reynolds explained.

"Oh, how sad," she said softly, scowling. *What kind of act could it be that had no speaking?*

Ezra continued, "Addie, would you show them to their dressing room? It's number six."

Using her cane for guidance, Addie stepped over to a rack on the wall upon which hung various keys. She counted over from the left, removed the key to number six, and then turned back toward the new guests. "Follow me, please."

As she exited confidently, Reynolds glanced at Ezra with an eyebrow raised, letting Ezra know he was impressed at her skills. Ezra smiled proudly. "I'll see you tonight, Charlie." The pair followed Addie.

Ezra turned back to his work as the three left. But they were not fully out the door when Patrick, a gangly, red-haired stagehand in his early twenties, burst into the room, out of breath.

"Ezra!" he exclaimed. "I've got one! Just listen to this," he chuckled. "It's about an Irishman, a priest, and a leprechaun…" Before he could say much more, two costumed showgirls, Mary and Bridgette, appeared in the doorway behind him.

"Not right now, Patrick. I've got bookwork to catch up on," he said, not looking up.

Patrick noticed the girls. "Oh, sorry, Guv. Uh…I guess I'll tell it to you later." He backed away as the girls entered—and he almost escaped.

"Oh, Patrick!" Ezra re-summoned Patrick, who poked his head back in the doorway, eyebrows raised quizzically. "See that the stage is well swept, will you? The dancers are complaining," Ezra ordered and turned back to his books.

"Sure thing, Guv." A crestfallen Patrick turned to exit.

Ezra took pity on him, offered a smile, and called after him as he left. "Hey, don't give up, Patrick. You'll make me laugh one of these days."

Patrick's exit from the office left behind smirks on the dancers.

To the girls, Ezra held out his upturned palms and cocked his head slightly while looking coyly at them as if to say, "Satisfied?"

Mary, the redhead, giggled as the two turned to leave.

"Close the door when you go," Ezra grumbled.

"Thank you, Ezra!" came their saccharine exclamation in unison as they walked out.

Addie led Reynolds and his companion down the stairs to the basement and straight to their dressing room. She unlocked the door and pushed it open. "Here you are. Number six. The washroom is two doors down."

Reynolds marveled at how Addie maneuvered so deftly, even gracefully, throughout the space, "Simply amazing, child. You do so well considering…"

"Considering what?" Addie asked. "Oh, you mean I'm blind." She shrugged. "I've always been this way. Here's the key." She held it out, and Reynolds took it. Then Addie stepped over and turned up the gaslights a notch. Fedor found himself desperately wanting to talk to her as a fellow non-ordinary person but held his tongue. Keeping his silence was a mandatory part of the act.

Reynolds couldn't help it and found himself asking Addie, "Miss Addie, wouldn't you like to be able to see if you could?"

"I don't know. I see things well enough," noted Addie somewhat flippantly, though it was a topic she didn't really want to think about. "I just don't use my eyes; that's what Rachel says. Is there anything else you need?"

"We have a trunk and a folded metal cage coming by separate carriage," Reynolds said.

"When it arrives Papa'll have it brought to you."

"That'll be fine, my dear," said Reynolds. "Thank you."

He and Fedor entered the spartan dressing room, and Addie moved toward the door.

"Who's Rachel?" muttered Fedor softly, reflexively. Reynolds immediately shot him a furious glance.

"What's that?" Addie asked.

"Um…who's Rachel?" Reynolds echoed, stepping in, clearing his throat, glowering at Fedor.

Addie answered matter-of-factly, "Oh…she's my teacher." With that, she went upstairs, not realizing the tense silence she had left behind.

Chapter Two

That same overcast afternoon, Rachel Darnay, a plain but well-groomed woman of thirty whose eyes seemed to smile even when she was at her most solemn, stood gazing steadfastly at the gaudy exterior of the Ruby Palace Theatre. She gathered her resolve and strode up the steps. As she approached the large, glass-paned entrance, William, a tall, uniformed doorman opened the door slightly and firmly recited, "The show doesn't start till 7:30, Miss. May I help you?"

"I need to speak with Ezra Alexander, please," replied Rachel in a no-nonsense manner. But then her face brightened when she noticed Addie not far away inside the lobby. "Addie!" she called out.

Addie approached, smiling, "Rachel? What're you doing here?"

"I need to discuss some things with your father," she explained.

"It's all right, William, she's my teacher," Addie told the doorman, whose expression softened.

"Welcome, Miss Rachel; come in," smiled William, opening the door wide.

Addie took Rachel's arm and turned her toward the corridor and stairs. "Papa's in his office, same as he always is. It's upstairs. This way." With her cane, she led Rachel down the corridor toward the rear stairs.

"Can I tell you about the dream I had?" Addie chatted.

Rachel smiled. "Was it a good one?"

"Oh yes!" Addie continued. "I dreamed I was listening to music that was so sweet and beautiful that it spun itself into marmalade."

"Delicious sounds, hmm? Sounds delicious! You *did* save me some…" Rachel always enjoyed sharing Addie's fantasies.

Addie chuckled. But hers wasn't the only laughter in the corridor. Female giggling was emanating from behind the closed office door. "That's Papa's office," Addie noted. Rachel stopped smiling. She adjusted her prim outfit and then, very deliberately, knocked on the door. The giggling subsided.

"Come in." Ezra's voice boomed from the other side of the door. As Rachel pushed the door open she discovered Ezra and the two showgirls, one of whom, Mary, was standing behind Ezra's chair looking over his shoulder as he scribbled on a piece of sheet music. When Ezra noticed his new visitor, he stood up, blushed, and pushed his hair back. "Rachel! This is a shock. We were just…uh, doing some rehearsing."

"I'm sorry to disturb you, Ezra, but I need to discuss something important with you…in private," she stated.

Addie took the hint, "I'll see you later, Rache." She turned back down the corridor.

"All right, Sweetie," replied Rachel, entering Ezra's office.

Ezra stammered, "Yes, uh, Mary, Bridgette, why don't you two run along and teach Addie this new song you've been working on? We'll pick this up later." He handed the sheet music to Mary and motioned her toward the door.

"Sure thing, Ezra," said Mary coolly as she stepped out of the office.

Bridgette was close behind. "See you later, Ezra."

In the corridor, the two dancers maneuvered past Addie. "So, what sort of song is it, Mary?" Addie asked as they passed her.

Mary halted only briefly. "Uh, listen, honey, I gotta get my makeup on."

Addie turned to the other girl, "Bridgette?"

"Yeah, me too. Some other time, Addie, huh?"

Addie got it. "Sure." The wind taken from her sails, she put her hands in her pockets and rediscovered the paper turtle she had intended to give to her father; at this moment she found herself wishing there was a tortoise shell that *she* could retreat into.

Ezra closed the door and returned to his desk. "So Rachel. What brings you to this 'den of iniquity?' I hope it's not my soul again. You know I already sold that."

Rachel wasn't smiling. "Ezra, please. Whatever differences you and I may have don't really matter at the moment. This concerns Addie."

The uneasy smile vanished from Ezra's lips. "Oh, what's she done?"

"It's nothing like that. It's what I'm doing—or going to do." Rachel took a deep breath. "You see, I've been offered a position managing a program for blind children at St. John's Hospital in Manchester."

"I see. Opportunity knocks," said Ezra, his brow starting to furl.

"It's a wonderful hospital, Ezra, and a chance to help lots of children. I don't see how I can ignore where the Lord is leading. But I have to be concerned about what this may do to Addie. She's had me all her life."

Ezra scratched his head. "You *are* the closest thing to a mother she's ever had…" The potential seriousness of Addie's situation without Rachel was beginning to dawn on him.

Rachel was getting a bit misty-eyed, but her voice didn't waver. "Yes, that was my promise to Annabelle before she died…But Addie has always been a joy, Ezra. She grows more like Annabelle every day. I would have cared for her purely out of Christian charity; you knew that. So I am truly grateful that you've always insisted on paying me as her teacher."

Ezra had to look away. "I don't know what I would have done without you all these years, Rachel."

"But now Addie is nearly grown, Ezra. I've taught her most everything I know how. Other children need help now, and I can give it to them. Addie's a strong girl. But when I leave, she is really going to need the strength of her father."

"What do you suggest?" Ezra asked.

"For now, give her all the comfort and love you can show her. Give her courage through your example," Rachel offered. The look in Ezra's eyes said it wasn't helping much.

"That's well and good to say. Rachel, you know I love Addie, more than anything. But I've also got a business to run here…

and what about her schooling?" Ezra's mind was starting to reel. He had always felt inadequate raising his daughter. Now, he feared for what would befall Addie in the absence of a strong, nurturing influence like Rachel.

"I'm sure you'll do what's absolutely best for her, Ezra." There was a pause as they both considered the implications of this change in their lives.

Ezra's thoughts returned to when Rachel had entered their lives, the darkness of Annabelle's passing, and the panic of being left on his own with a mewling infant. Yet, like a gift from above, Rachel had suddenly been there, scooping the child into her arms and, in so doing, removing myriad questions and burdens from his grieving heart. And when, sometime later, it became evident that the young child was blind, Rachel never missed a step. She not only dove headlong into providing the special care that Addie needed but reassurance and comfort for his soul as well. He reflected that those times seemed an eternity ago, yet the fear threatened to return.

Ezra broke the silence, "How soon are you leaving?"

"In two weeks, as soon as I can get things in order here," Rachel stated, looking down at her fidgeting hands.

"When are you going to tell Addie?" asked Ezra glumly.

Rachel suppressed a sigh. "Tomorrow, after Worship Service," she replied.

Unknown to Rachel and Ezra, Addie stood just outside the office door in the shadows of the corridor. She had heard their every word, her eyes fully demonstrating that, though they might not possess sight, they were fully capable of tears and the sorrow of a girl whose world was disintegrating.

Not only had Rachel led the infant Addie from her darkness into the skills of a fully functional girl, but she had been her sole teacher and closest friend for all of her twelve years. Addie might as well have heard that she was about to become an orphan. The loss of such a loving and motherly mentor would be unimaginable.

As the evening curtain time came nearer, Addie slowly made her way in silence along the corridor and down the clanging metal utility stairs. At the last stair, she found she had to pause— her hands were trembling, and dread gripped her chest, making it difficult even to breathe. A cigar-chomping baggy-pants comic, a ballerina, and several stagehands scurried past Addie, avoiding collision but paying her no notice. The baying of the stage manager echoed up the stairway, "Curtain in one minute! Madame Lezinski and the Guillory Twins onstage. Curtain in one minute!"

Reynolds and Fedor were coming up the stairs from the dressing rooms, passing Addie as they reached the stage level. Only Fedor noticed her distress, and his own throat began to tighten as he witnessed her sorrow. He had seen tears before. And Lord knows he had shed his own fair share. But this was different. As they passed near Addie, an overwhelming, searing sense of abandonment and loss washed over and consumed him, something far deeper than merely observing someone's tears. He had never felt this sort of connection to another person before. Yet his inability to console this girl frustrated and disheartened him. Fedor held back slightly from Reynolds' brisk gait, hoping to birth an idea of how he might comfort her. But Reynolds' insistent rope beckoned him on and into the wing of the theatre's stage left.

Addie, unaware of these events, continued down the corridor toward a door that led to the booth that housed the theatre's lime-light spotlight. Its brilliant light was one of the first of its kind to operate in Liverpool during those days before electricity, and it was an intense source of pride for Ezra. There in that booth she knew she would find Patrick, her friend whose duty it was to operate this scalding behemoth, following the performers with its beam whether they pranced or shuffled around the stage. So he would be busy, and she could withdraw into this space as a turtle into its shell. Despite the bustle, clamour, and applause of this theatre world, all Addie could anticipate was a life of imminent emptiness, with no one to share her innermost hopes, dreams, and fears.

She paused for a minute in the corridor and tried to scold herself, saying Rachel would be going off to to what God had prepared her to do, and she would be happy in her new role. Addie knew she should be glad for Rachel. And she *had* to be happy for all the other children who would soon benefit, as she had, from Rachel's patient teaching. Yes, she dutifully scolded herself. But she was still sad.

As all was being finally readied to begin the evening's performance, the last straggling audience members were shuffling through the lobby. Among them was an impressive gentleman who entered the theatre just as the downbeat of the overture began. The mustachioed fellow in evening clothes, sporting a Homburg hat and a waist-length satin-lined cape, strode resolutely up to the ticket taker, then dropped his hat and cloak at the check counter, and headed down the theatre's aisle toward the dress-circle seats. Though no one seemed to notice, he was entirely over-dressed compared to most of the house's more working-class clientele. The gentleman found his aisle seat next to some of those working patrons and settled in. But it wasn't long before the slightly shabby fellow next to him sniffed his nose at the gentleman's cologne, smiled, and gave a nudge with his elbow. "Ooh! Smellin' grand, Mate!" The gentleman closed his eyes briefly and steadfastly remained facing forward, apparently having determined not to offer the dignity of a response.

Chapter Three

Addie, at last, entered the isolated and quieter realm of the spotlight booth, the domain of someone she could comfortably be around for the evening.

"Addie!" Patrick exclaimed. "Where've you been? You never miss Saturday nights."

"I've been around," came the low-key reply.

"I saved your favourite stool for you," Patrick offered, knowing she liked sitting next to one of the booth's ports where she could hear everything on stage. "Hey, what's the matter, Kiddo?" Before she could reply, however, the overture ended. "Oops, there's my cue. Excuse me." He opened the douser on his device, and the intense beam splashed onto a stage-right easel containing a stack of placards. Showgirl Bridgette, in a silken costume that ended in knee-length bloomers, strutted out with drum accompaniment and applause mixed with catcalls to remove the graphical front card, revealing another proclaiming: "Madame Lezinski, the Irish Nightingale."

Patrick tracked his spotlight with Bridgette as she exited the stage, then proceeded to pick up Madame Lezinski, a matronly soprano who glided toward stage centre in an elegant velvet gown. "I like her," Patrick noted. "She doesn't move around very much." With the five-piece orchestra's four-bar introduction finishing just as she hit her mark, Madame Lezinski then launched into an overly sincere rendition of Gilbert and Sullivan's "Poor Wandering One" from *Pirates of Penzance*.

Addie paid little attention. Her mind swam with memories of a childhood filled with learning and growing under Rachel's kind tutelage. Without Rachel, her world would be a different place. Papa was consumed with running the business and, though he loved and even doted on her, really had no idea about the proper ways to raise a daughter, especially one verging on womanhood. He and Addie would soon be adrift, apart from the anchor that Rachel had always provided. It all seemed bleak to Addie—but a glimmer of an idea was beginning to grow in her imagination, and the corners of her mouth began to turn up. She might even be able to help more than just herself, but she didn't have a great deal of time.

The orchestra gave a final flourish as Madame Lezinski finished her song and took her bow to tepid applause and a few whistles. As she strode off the stage, her bustle took on a life of its own. The main curtain came down, and showgirl Bridgette returned to reveal the placard for the next act: "The Dog-Faced Boy."

Patrick perked up. "I've wondered what this act was gonna be about." Upon the completion of Bridgette's bass-drum-enhanced stage right exit, the orchestra played an introduction for a tuxedoed Reynolds, who quickly took his place in front of the curtain to polite applause, looking out over the gas footlights with Patrick's limelight lending him a brilliant halo.

When the musical intro concluded, he began to speak: "Ladies and gentlemen. My name is Charles Reynolds. I come to you straight from the great and dark Kostroma forest of central Russia. There, my colleagues and I discovered wild creatures so fantastic that, were I not to witness them with my own eyes, I would scarcely believe our tale myself. Yet, despite an immense and Homeric struggle, we have brought one of these unique beings back here to civilization that you also, ladies and gentlemen, may see and believe."

Patrick whispered to Addie, attempting to cheer her up, "I saw this bloke backstage, and judging by his breath, I'll bet the closest he's ever been to Russia is the inside of a bottle of vodka." Addie did indeed manage a hint of a smile.

Reynolds continued, "…It is with great pride, therefore, that we present for your education and amazement, and with the permission of the Tsar himself, ladies and gentlemen…The amazing Dog-Faced Boy!"

The curtain parted majestically with a vaguely Russian musical fanfare to reveal a dramatically lit Fedor, clad only in satin boxer shorts and a matching collar, squatting on a small platform, snarling and growling as fiercely as his slight frame would allow. Long, shiny hair covered virtually every inch of his body and several stout ropes attached to his collar restrained him. Addie winced at all the growling.

"He surely is a hairy brute," noted Patrick.

Reynolds carried on, "Although you may note his keen resemblance to a simple domestic terrier, this young creature was a prince in his world, among his kind."

Suddenly, a heckler stood up in the crowd, "Yeah, I'll bet he was a prince all right…Here Prince, here boy!" Peals of laughter echoed through the theatre.

Fedor snarled all the louder—it was all he *could* do. It was the role he was playing, and he had to consider the greater good it did to provide a living not only for himself and Charlie but for the theatre's staff as well. So a brief indignity, a little humiliation was perhaps a fair exchange for the blessings that resulted. Some day, perhaps it would be different. But for now, this was his lot.

Reynolds attempted to ignore the interruption. "Local legends informed our party of an entire race of these creatures, a society closely intertwined with that of the mountain timber wolf. Our party struggled valiantly with a beast we were told was this specimen's father, a creature twice his size with three times the ferocity. Alas, our attempt to bring not one but two of these amazing creatures to your world was doomed to failure. For the larger creature was more than five mere mortal men could subdue."

The heckler stood up again and shouted, "Bollocks! I say. It's a fake! Any bloke can paste hair on a lad!"

Reynolds had a ready response, "My friend, I'm glad you mentioned that. It gives us an opportunity to prove for all our spectators the veracity of this amazing tale. Sir, step up here to the platform if you will…"

"Who, m-me?" stammered the heckler, a balding man with a greying mustache and well-worn clothing. Although he tried to decline, the remainder of the crowd goaded him into compliance with Reynolds' offer.

Reynolds called offstage, "Gentlemen if you would be so kind…" Two burly stagehands emerged and forcefully subdued Fedor into a prone position as the heckler timidly climbed the steps to the stage. The boisterous crowd wildly cheered the heckler. Hat in hand, he bashfully grinned and looked out past the footlights to his mates in the audience. "Sir, if you would please," continued Reynolds, "confirm for yourself that this specimen of a throwback to wild primitive man is no mere fabrication. Ascertain that any and all of his astonishing hairy mane is as firmly rooted as yours and mine," Reynolds continued as the heckler hesitantly made his way across the stage.

"You mean, like, pull on it?" the heckler asked. The audience tittered.

"Certainly, pull on it, my friend, to convince yourself and your neighbors of this creature's authenticity. Don't worry; as you can see, he is fully restrained," Reynolds urged.

"Well, all right…if you say so," stammered the heckler.

Addie's stomach churned in horror. "That's so mean! Why do they treat him so?"

There was an anticipatory silence as the heckler cautiously stepped over to Fedor, pausing momentarily to figure what piece of hair to grasp, accompanied by increasingly rowdy taunts from the crowd. Finally, he selected a tuft on Fedor's forehead. He gave it a good tug, causing Fedor to let out a howl, which in turn sent the heckler scurrying back to his seat. As he pushed his way down the row, he called out to his neighbors, "It's real by thunder! Blessed holy mother!"

The audience rolled with laughter. The only one not laughing was Fedor—but the heckler hadn't truly injured him. In fact, Fedor had learned to appreciate the reactions his howls brought. It meant the guests were being entertained. And that, as Charlie always told him, was his job.

Reynolds continued: "And now, ladies and gentlemen, a brief demonstration of the beginnings of domestication of this amazing creature. Gentlemen…"

The orchestra struck up a waltz as the stagehands removed all of Fedor's restraints except for a long velvet rope leash. The other end of it they handed to Reynolds, who picked up a small buggy whip with his other hand. With one crack of the whip, Fedor slowly rose from all-fours to a standing position accompanied by a salutary chord from the orchestra, which in turn precipitated applause. Another whip crack, and Fedor did a handstand—to more applause and took a couple of steps using his hands—more applause.

Reynolds continued to prod Fedor through a series of minor acrobatics, one of which involved balancing a large bone vertically on his nose. After a count of two, Fedor grabbed the bone and began to gnaw on it fiercely with a theatrical flair.

As Fedor looked up from his bone, however, he spotted a distant Addie, as if framed in a picture, standing in the open port of the spotlight booth, her image seeming to him to float in the darkness. Sullenness still greyed her features. An emptiness in his abdomen grabbed him as he once more felt her sadness and his own seeming inability to do anything about it. What's worse, he sensed, the humiliating spectacle of this performance was making her even more sad.

But a crack of the whip and a glowering glance from Reynolds rudely snapped Fedor back into the act. The stagehands brought on and positioned a mounted four-foot horizontal bar whose ends Reynolds set aflame. Another whip crack and Fedor backed up two steps, then, rushing forward, performed a hand-spring over the flaming bar, neatly landing on all-fours on the small padded stand where he had begun the presentation. Applause thundered from the house.

But the velvet rope had somehow detached itself from his collar in the acrobatic action. Unaware, Reynolds began taking his bows. Fedor didn't know what to do. He knew where the act had to end. He was, after all, a "fierce beast" and had to be restrained. After a moment of indecision, he determined to make the scene right. He quickly reached down, grabbed the rope, and dutifully re-attached it to his collar just as the curtain was clos-ing. A few titters rang out in the crowd, but the applause still echoed loud and long.

Ezra knocked on the door of dressing room six in the afterglow of the evening's performance.

"Come in," came the response.

Ezra pushed the door open to reveal Reynolds sitting at the dressing table. An empty metal cage about six feet by four was tucked into one corner of the room, containing a small cot, a stool, and a dish of water.

"Charlie! Congratulations," Ezra exclaimed. "The crowd really ate it up. And we had a full house." Then he noted the half-empty bottle sitting next to Charlie. "Oh," he smiled, holding up a bottle of celebratory Champagne that he'd brought along. "Looks like you won't be needing this."

"Nonsense, Ezra!" Reynolds said as he pulled himself to standing and grabbed the bottle from him. "Come, join me!"

"I can't right now, Charlie. I have to take care of some things, closing up for the night, you know. Um…Where's your…partner?"

"Oh, he's in the loo. He'll be right along," Reynolds smiled sheepishly.

Ezra glanced in the direction of the washroom. "I hope that's not going to cause problems with the other performers. Well, tell him congratulations for me. I need to be running along," Ezra said, stepping toward the door. "It looks like this is going to be a good run."

No sooner had Ezra wandered off than Fedor emerged from the backstage bathroom, preceded by two other performers who hurried to get away from the human oddity, even though he kept a towel over his head, minimizing, as always, his exposure to the public eye. While drying his ample hair, he approached the dressing room and looked in. From the doorway, he sighed as he beheld Reynolds, a bottle of whiskey at his side, still seated at the dressing table.

A tense moment later, Reynolds slowly turned to behold his charge. Suddenly, he raised his voice angrily, "You broke character tonight! You broke character! What goes through that fur-bearing head of yours?"

"But I didn't mean…" Fedor sputtered, realizing the storm that lay ahead.

"Doesn't this act mean anything to you?" Reynolds slurred. "You want to blow the whole enterprise? You want to cut off all that nice money I've been sending your mother?"

"I'm sorry, Charlie, I just saw…"

Reynolds rose quickly and stumbled to close the door with a loud thud. "I'll teach you sorry, you ungrateful…" He reeled around and back-handed Fedor with such force that it slammed his slight frame against the wall.

Fedor was nearly in tears. "It won't happen again, Charlie. Please don't…"

"You *bet* it won't happen again." Another slap landed. "There's a reminder."

Fedor begged, "Don't Charlie, please…please…"

At that moment, another knock came on the door. Fedor continued to cower in the corner, quietly whimpering.

"Who is it?" barked Reynolds.

"Message for Mr. Charles Reynolds," came the reply. Reynolds opened the door to find Walter Hodge, the building caretaker, offering an envelope. With the acrid smell of alcohol emanating from the room, Walter wouldn't linger any longer than necessary. Reynolds accepted the message with a muttered thanks and closed the door as Walter retreated. He then awkwardly slumped back into the dressing table's chair and fumbled with the envelope.

Fedor remained silent in the corner, watching as Charlie shakily retrieved the contents: a business card and a note. For a long moment, Charlie stared at the papers. After an initial reading, he looked away briefly and ran his hand over his head, trying to understand through his alcohol fog what was happening and what it meant. Then he read it again, and gradually, a vague smile curled on his lips. He turned to Fedor.

"Get up, Lad." He tucked the papers into his vest pocket and tried to clear his head. "We may have an opportunity coming our way."

A wary Fedor slowly stood as Bad Charlie seemed to be prematurely subsiding, giving way to the Civil Charlie that he knew more commonly.

"A man wants to meet with me tomorrow—a very important man in our business, to discuss 'a proposal'. I don't want to get ahead of ourselves, but this could be stupendous for us!" He then gave an apprehensive Fedor an affectionate slap on the shoulder. Fedor did his best to smile. As cruel as Charlie could be, he was still Fedor's only link to normal society. He knew these days wouldn't last forever, and the newly delivered message was evidence of that. So he contented himself with staying alert while continuing to dream of the great "Some Day."

In the spotlight booth, Patrick was packing up gear and performing maintenance on the limelight instrument in preparation for the following day's performance as Addie sat nearby folding paper. She had been silent much of the evening but remained there throughout the performance as she usually did. As Patrick applied some graphite lubricant to the spotlight's iris, he tried to get Addie to open up. "So what's gnawing at you, Kiddo? You've been acting like you lost your best friend."

Addie remained silent for a moment, then muttered, "I have, Patrick."

"What? What are you talking about? I'm still here, aren't I?" he kidded as he wrapped up the flexible gas line and stowed it.

"You're my friend, Patrick," she smiled slightly. "But you're not my *best* friend."

"Well then…am I moving up at least?"

"It's Rachel, Patrick. She's going away." Addie wiped a descending tear.

Patrick looked up from his work with shock on his face. "Your teacher? You two have been thick as fleas your whole life! What's gonna happen?"

"I don't know, Patrick." She morosely put her paper down and bowed her head. Rachel had always been the one with whom Addie could share her innermost troubles, and she seemed to possess an inexhaustible reservoir of solutions to almost any problem. Addie couldn't conceive of anyone replacing her.

Patrick was stymied. But tentatively, he offered, "I…I'm sure it'll work out somehow. There's lots of us around here that'll still be your mates." He put the final touches on his duties and stood up. "C'mon, Kiddo, grab your cane, and let's get you home. Something good will happen tomorrow. Just wait. Hey, what's that you've been working on?"

She stood and placed her completed paper-folding project into his hand. "This is for you," she said as they neared the door.

Patrick looked down in his hand to discover a whimsical origami dog.

"Hey, that Dog-Boy act must've impressed you. This is beautiful, Addie."

"I just wonder what it's like to be half dog and half boy," Addie mused. "He must be very lonely." She yawned as she took Patrick's arm for guidance.

"Well, maybe you can dream about him tonight and give him company," smiled Patrick. The two continued down the stairs of the now-quiet theatre and out into the cool air of the summer night, heading towards the Alexander home just a few blocks away.

Unlike the other floors of the theatre, its basement was not quiet that night. Charlie Reynolds' snores echoed down the corridor. He had fallen asleep hunched over the dressing table, the three-quarters empty whiskey bottle still clutched in one hand. Across the room, Fedor crouched in the corner, nodding off.

But Fedor woke with a start. After gathering his bearings, he decided he'd had enough. Stretching, he stood up, approached Charlie, and gingerly removed the bottle from his grasp, slinking away to hide it in a store room several doors away. Returning to the dressing room, he attempted to rouse Reynolds, first gently, then firmly. "Come on, Charlie. Wake up. We need to get to the hotel," he urged. Fedor knew he couldn't exactly check in to the hotel by himself with the results that he knew his appearance often elicited, even with his hooded cloak. Nor could he really leave his partner behind. If he did, it would certainly not go well in the morning. Charlie was terrible when he was drinking. But without the drink, he took protective care of Fedor. So it was in Fedor's best interest to take care of Charlie. The snores continued, however. Fedor moved on to a more strident shaking. All to no avail. Charlie was definitely out.

Fedor proceeded to carefully lower Charlie to the floor so that he wouldn't tumble over and injure himself. He removed Charlie's shoes and placed one under his head, covering Charlie with his coat for warmth in the cool of the basement dressing room. Then Fedor himself settled in on the cot in the metal cage with a pile of rags that he had scrounged for a pillow. The cage and its props were usually just for appearances. But tonight, they would be put to use.

As Fedor lay there, he began to reflect on the day's events and wondered if his life would ever get better. He had always determined to make the best of whatever circumstances he found himself in. But still, he found himself asking, *Is this all there is? What did he have to look forward to?* Perhaps the message that Charlie received would make a difference. Charlie seemed to think so. Fedor comforted himself with this thought, pulled his traveling cloak over himself, and encamped till morning.

Chapter Four

Rachel, adorned in her Sunday best, approached the leaded glass front door of the Alexander home. It was a splendid Victorian house and a fitting testament to the accomplishments of Ezra Alexander. The door opened as Rachel came near, revealing Addie.

"Good morning, Addie," greeted Rachel. "All ready?"

"Morning, Rachel. Let's go." Addie closed the door behind her. Rachel placed Addie's hand on her own arm as they made their way down the steps to the waiting horse and buggy. "No thanks," Addie said, pulling her hand away. "I can make it all right." And, using her cane, she did.

Rachel smiled, "That's my girl." They climbed into the Stanhope buggy and were on their way to the small country chapel that occupied their Sunday mornings.

.   .   .

The din of the city gradually gave way to the sound of birds and rustling trees in a more wooded countryside as the one-horse buggy left the heart of town behind. The absence of urban clattering only emphasized the silence on board. Rachel glanced over at a pensive Addie whose head was down. "You're awfully quiet this morning."

"Rachel, do you think Papa will go to hell because he doesn't go to chapel with us?"

Rachel smiled, then sighed and thought for a moment. "I prefer to think God has his own special plan for your father. Why do you ask?"

"In the Kingdom of Heaven, when I can see with my eyes, I want to be able to see him."

This kind of earnest innocence had always endeared Addie to Rachel. "I'm sure you will, Sweetheart," she affirmed.

After a moment, Addie blurted, "Do you think he's handsome?"

Rachel peered at Addie, trying to fathom what was going on in that imagination of hers. "…Yes…," she at last admitted to herself softly. "I suppose I do."

Addie's lips smiled in satisfaction, and they rode on in silence.

The picturesque stone chapel nestled itself under a trio of large shade trees; inside, the benches were nearly full of the hundred or so souls that the church could contain. Addie and Rachel occupied their customary places in the third pew.

The pastor was continuing his series of sermons from the book of Job: "'…and I alone am left behind to tell thee.' said the servant. Yet despite all of this, my friends, the loss of his family, the destruction of his property, and even when his friends turned on him, the patriarch Job remained upright and righteous in the eyes of God. We are to *submit* to our trials, dear ones, and continue to worship God, not because we see the reasons for those trials, but because God wills them and has his own reasons which we are to trust…"

Addie sat stoically, absorbing and trying to process the pastor's words in light of the approaching times of friendlessness that seemed to be upon her; she couldn't help getting tense as those thoughts washed over her. Job's losses certainly seemed to echo her own as she prepared to board the ship of adulthood with no one to help her navigate the rocks and the storms.

"Our faith, Beloved," continued the pastor, "is a burst of brilliant flowers springing up in the arid desert of our lives. Cherish these orphaned blooms of faith that God has provided, dear ones.

Water them, encourage them, and they will fill your parched heart with colour, celebration, and joy."

With the last verse of the last hymn finished, the service was complete. Addie and Rachel filed out with the parishioners to greet the pastor at the chapel door, thanking him for his sermon, while the pump organ played its postlude, "It's very good to see you this morning, Miss Rachel, Miss Addie," Pastor Fisher smiled, shaking their hands.

"Yes," said Addie, her somberness surfacing as she continued walking using her cane, "It is very good to see…"

Rachel caught up with Addie and studied her expression, trying to discern what was troubling her as they walked.

The two arrived at the buggy and began climbing in. Addie stopped short, her dark clouds parting slightly.

"Why do I smell muffins?" she asked.

"I brought lunch," Rachel explained. "Would you like to go on a picnic?"

Addie smiled, but not as broadly as she might. She settled into her seat. "You have to ask?"

Rachel sighed coyly and straight-faced. "I suppose I should know better. I'll drop the food off at the boarding house and take you on home…"

Addie gave Rachel a playful shove. They both laughed as the horse led the buggy on down the road into the countryside.

In a grassy meadow, Addie and Rachel, having spread their feast in the grass near a grove of trees, were just finishing their meal. Rachel patted her mouth with a napkin. She settled back, gazed at the sky, and contentedly inhaled the perfume of the grasses and flowers. "What a glorious day this turned out to be!"

"Tell me, Rachel," Addie pleaded, "Tell me what it looks like."

Rachel laid back and began waxing playfully poetic. "Well, the clouds…are like vast pillows drifting across the sky. The trees…they're like silent worshipers, arms held forever heavenward, praising God. And the sun…it's like a warm hearth fire that all Creation tries to snuggle up to."

Addie settled back also and enjoyed the touch of a breeze and the sun's warmth on her face. There was a peaceful calm as they basked in the summer sunshine of the English countryside.

"Rachel?" Addie broke the silence. "Why haven't you ever married?"

Caught a bit off guard, Rachel retreated to a pat answer, "Well, no gentleman has ever asked me."

"None at all?" Addie pressed.

"I don't suppose too many gentlemen find me very attractive."

Addie became indignant and sat up, "What's wrong with them? You're a wonderful person."

"Men look on outside things, Addie. God is the one who looks on our hearts," Rachel explained patiently, perhaps attempting to reassure herself.

"Sometimes I'm glad to be blind rather than be like that…" Addie fumed.

"I'm glad you are who you are," Rachel smiled. Then she took a deep breath and sighed to herself, knowing she had to get this over with. "Addie, I have something I need to tell…"

Addie interrupted, "What about Papa? Did you ever think of marrying him?"

"What?" Rachel puzzled. "Why Addie, what *ever* are you talking about?"

"Well…if you were to marry him then…then you wouldn't have to *leave* us…Oh, Rachel!" Addie burst into tears and collapsed in Rachel's arms, sobbing. It finally became clear to Rachel.

"Oh, so that's what this is all about. You must've heard us talking yesterday. Oh, Addie…I'm so sorry. Shhh…" She stroked Addie's hair and wiped her tears. Rachel herself found it hard to hold back tears. Words were of little use now. All she could do was hold tightly to Addie and try to comfort her. She, too, was becoming more apprehensive of what might befall Addie in her absence. Sometimes, she admitted, she needed Addie's bright and unique insights almost as much as Addie needed her guidance. And when she had gone, would she ever see Addie again? Would Addie even speak to her? But she couldn't be thinking this way. Her path was set. These thoughts shouldn't be hectoring her now.

Charlie Reynolds stood before the dressing room mirror, adjusting his bow tie. He moved on to organize what little hair he had, using a brush. Fedor sat on his stool watching. Reynolds pulled a tarnished silver watch from his lower vest pocket and noted: "Almost two o'clock, Lad. I'd better get going." He pulled on his coat. "This meeting could change both of our lives." He grabbed his bowler. "Wish me luck, Lad."

"Where are you meeting him, Charlie?" asked Fedor.

"The Crafty Raven Pub just down the way a bit. Now lay low, Lad, and I'll see you in a while." He turned. "Figure the longer I'm gone, the better the deal," Charlie winked and headed out.

"Good luck, Charlie," Fedor called as the door closed.

Fedor didn't understand these business things. But if Charlie thought it was a good opportunity, he had little choice but to trust him.

Not much later, Patrick was making his way down London Street toward the theatre to prepare for the evening's performance when he noticed someone who looked like Reynolds entering the Crafty Raven just up ahead. As he passed the window of the tavern, he paused, confirming it was, in fact, Charlie, and observed that he was shaking hands with a well-dressed gentleman in a Homburg hat.

Patrick decided to stay and watch for a bit. Whereas Charlie was both smiling broadly and animated in his gestures, the well-dressed gentleman was convivial in his body language but much more subdued. The gentleman's gesture invited Charlie to sit down. As they took their seats, he pulled out a vertically folded document and placed it before Charlie. The gentleman kept speaking as Charlie read the document. His lips were the only part of the gentleman's anatomy that seemed to be moving. At length, he reached into his vest and withdrew a fountain pen, which he handed to Charlie. No longer smiling as broadly, Charlie didn't take the pen and seemed to be asking questions. After the gentleman responded, Charlie nodded and picked up the pen. The meeting seemed to be civil enough, but Patrick shook his head. He didn't understand why Ezra trusted that bloke. Who knew what he was up to? But Patrick slung his burlap lunch sack over his shoulder and continued on to work.

. . .

The door to dressing room six cracked open slightly, and Fedor peered out into the corridor. It was early yet, with half a dozen hours before show time, so the theatre was yet quiet, only just beginning to show signs of life. He knew that, with his meeting taking place in the pub, Charlie would likely be there for hours. Fedor decided to explore this quiet world, stepping tentatively out into the corridor. He left his cumbersome cloak in the dressing room, not only because he was tired of it, but because his appearance without the cloak more or less assured that he would be left to his own in this expedition.

His assumption of peaceful wandering was almost immediately shattered by the agitation and rapid scurrying of two passing singers—but they did indeed leave him alone. He headed up the stairs. However, the next floor up was the main floor, home to the stage and lobby areas, and he had already seen quite enough of them. So the mezzanine floor beckoned.

He resolutely climbed the next flight of stairs. Upon reaching the landing, he found that this new floor seemed quieter than even the basement and a bit dimmer. Unlike the main lobby, whose floor was polished marble, this lobby was covered with lush carpet, and he liked how his feet sank into the softness. The ceiling was arched and culminated in a single central skylight, surrounded by classical murals of nymphs, minotaurs, and satyrs in rolling green landscapes. He took heart in the fact that, like him, the figures in the paintings did not represent everyday humanity. Fedor marveled at the deftness of whoever had painted such a large and beautiful work.

To the left and straight ahead were the balcony access tunnels, which opened out to the auditorium and led to the balcony seats. But in the rear of this mezzanine lobby, Fedor's eye found a relatively obscure door, with no label, in a shadowed corner, so unassuming it seemed ripe for exploration. He unhurriedly traversed the lobby's luxurious burgundy carpeting while admiring the crystals adorning the unlit chandeliers above his head. Arriving at the plain white-painted door, he gently tried the handle. To his surprise—it opened.

SCALA
ROMEO
JULIET

Chapter Five

As Fedor slowly pushed open the door, he had to pause to allow his eyes to accustom to the dim and dusty space. A shaft of sunlight streamed in from a small high window, stabbing the darkness, but where it fell he could not yet observe for all the silhouetted objects obscuring his view. But he began to understand that this was some manner of prop and scenery storage where artifacts from past theatrical fantasies slept until their time to shine in the limelight might arrive once more.

From beyond the walls came the faint, muffled sounds of a piano and distant voices rehearsing in the main auditorium. A giant rabbit head from an Easter pageant looked down on him from one wall. A red velvet sleigh was piled with spears and glittery banners. Rolled-up backdrops of myriad fantastical locales occupied one corner, while chairs and tables from every time and land were stacked everywhere. *Papier mâché* angels were haphazardly piled atop a flower-covered chariot. Various banners and posters proclaiming theatrical wonders covered every wall. It was all here: reminders and tokens of glories past.

Fedor found himself admiring a mannequin figure of a tuxedoed gentleman. He stared at it until a nearby mirror caught his attention, reflecting his own gaze back at him. Wincing at the sight, he grabbed the edge of the mirror and turned it away, but it gave out a wooden creak as he did so.

"Who's there?" a female voice called out of the depths of darkness, startling Fedor.

"It…it's I…Fedor," he offered as he moved around the objects to gain a view of the voice's source. Suddenly, he saw Addie, sitting in a small splash of sunlight, curled up in the corner of a once-grand and velveted throne, looking positively angelic.

"Do I know you?" she asked.

"No, I'm afraid you don't quite know me," he admitted, his mind racing, searching for words that wouldn't make her afraid, or, worse yet, sad. "I…um, was looking for Charlie Reynolds," he continued, trying to buy himself time to think.

"He's not in here. Do you know Mr. Reynolds?" Addie asked.

"He's my boss. I-uh, help him take care of the dog-faced boy." There—he had chosen his path. Perhaps he could get her to accept him for himself if she didn't assume him to be some sort of hairy monster.

Addie perked up. "The audience seemed to really like the dog-faced boy. Do you train him?"

"Sometimes," dissembled Fedor. "But mostly it's Mr. Reynolds. Sometimes, though, when Charlie has had too much to drink, he hits him…and even me if I'm not careful."

Addie gasped. "I *knew* I didn't like that man."

Fedor moved a bit closer. "So I have to look after Dog-Boy when that happens." The rehearsals in the auditorium had seemingly concluded, and a dusty silence reigned. Fedor looked around. "This is such a strange dark place to hide a royal face such as yours, Your Highness," he noted as he studied the room.

"Highness? Oh, you mean the throne…" Addie blushed and smiled. "The darkness doesn't bother me, of course. This is my thinking place. My name's Addie."

"I've seen you around the theatre. You've been rather melancholy lately." Then he noticed the streaks on her cheeks. "And you've even shed some tears. What makes you so unhappy, Miss Addie?"

A sigh welled up inside Addie, "Rachel, my teacher. She's… going away."

Fedor handed her a handkerchief from his pocket and pulled up a nearby stool. "She must be very special to bring on such heartache at the mere thought of her leaving."

"She's my closest friend in the whole world. She's helped me get through everything." Addie sniffed.

"Ah, now, you may find that you have more friends than you know," he gently chided.

"Oh, you don't understand. Nobody understands."

"Is that why you came in here, away from everyone?"

Addie nodded. Then she admitted, "I used to play here when I was little. I loved the smell of perfume and greasepaint; this place reminded me of songs and laughing. Now…I come here when I'm…feeling sad."

"Feeling sad…hmmm…" he paused. "In my kingdom, of course, *that* wouldn't be allowed," Fedor asserted, attempting to spark her imagination.

"Kingdom? What do you mean?" she laughed nervously.

"I wouldn't expect you to believe me. But I actually used to be a prince...I *am* a prince. Of a land called Ziymia."

"I notice you do have a bit of an accent," she admitted. "Where is Ziymia?"

Fedor leaned closer and lowered his voice to a near-whisper, "It's oh, so far away...and yet much closer than you might think."

Addie was becoming intrigued and straightened herself up. "What's it like there?"

Fedor glanced around. "It's something like this place, your Thinking Place, but as big as all imagination. It's as warm as a down comforter and as fresh as snowflakes on your tongue. You would love it there, Miss Addie. The trees grow gumdrops; on holidays gravity is optional, and in the mornings all the birds make sounds like musical laughter."

"It all sounds so wonderful I can almost see it!" Addie said.

"I can tell, Miss Addie, that you see a great many things with your heart that others will never see, even with their eyes."

Addie blushed and fidgeted with her fingers.

Seeing her discomfort, he decided to change the subject. "So tell me, Addie: what is your favourite dessert?"

She didn't have to think about it. "Cherry trifle." Just saying the words brought a smile to her lips.

"That's our national food! You must already be a citizen of Ziymia."

Addie laughed but then turned her head away, embarrassed slightly. "I...I've never been outside of Liverpool."

"Oh, but I'm sure in this, your magnificent Thinking Place, and in your nightly dreams, that you have traveled to many a wondrous and fanciful place," Fedor noted.

He stepped over to the tuxedoed mannequin and removed a

ring from its smallest finger; then approached Addie. "Hold out your right hand," he instructed. When she complied, he gently placed the ring on Addie's middle finger.

"What's this?" she laughed nervously. "It fits so perfectly."

"Of course it fits perfectly. It's your royal signet ring. I hereby declare under the powers of my office as Fedor, prince of Ziymia, that you, Addie—uh…?"

"Alexander!"

"…Addie Alexander are designated as Royal Princess of the land of Ziymia with all the honors and privileges that pertain thereto."

Addie giggled. "Me? A real princess?"

"We all await your commands, Your Highness."

"I would love to go to Ziymia," exulted Addie. Then her brow furrowed slightly, "But why are you here? What brings a prince like you to Liverpool?"

Fedor had to think for a moment. This had to be good. "My father, King Frederick, sent me on a mission to obtain help from the outside world for some of our people." Her rapt interest only served to fuel and inspire Fedor on to further tales. "We have a province, in Ziymia, a village really, where many of our blind people live. And they're struggling; they need help that we don't know how to give. It's very unfortunate."

Addie replied reflexively, "Could I help? I've been blind all my life. I could teach them things!" she enthused.

"Oh, that would be wonderful, Miss Addie," lamented Fedor, "But you see, I don't know how to get back to Ziymia."

"What? Why not?"

"Our maps were lost. Our expedition set out with two carriages, myself and three others, along with two soldiers. Almost as soon as we crossed outside our homeland's border we were set upon by marauders, highwaymen looking to rob us. We had some money, not a lot, and they took that, but they also killed some of my companions."

Addie's face clenched in horror.

Fedor continued, "I think at least one of the soldiers escaped to report back to my Father. But I don't know. In all the scuffle, our maps disappeared. And Ziymia doesn't appear on any maps I see from other countries."

"Oh, how frustrating! Fedor!" gasped Addie.

"And, then, when the bandits determined that I was Ziymia's prince, they decided to hold me for ransom."

Fedor was beginning to enjoy the wild tales he heard coming from his own mouth.

"They held me for a week," he continued, "But, being bandits, they weren't the cleverest of fellows. They finally figured out that they didn't have any way of reaching my father —or anyone else--to make demands. So then they decided they could be raiding other travelers instead of wasting their time with me, so they sold me as a laborer to a traveling fair that was passing through the area."

"How awful!" Addie sighed sympathetically.

"It sounds awful. And sometimes it was. But there were some kindly people in that fair that took me under their wing and taught me a lot of things that a prince would never come to know otherwise. So, even though I was homesick, I was grateful to be learning things of the world.

"I toured with that fair all over Europe, saw all sorts of new places and people. One of those people was this fellow Charlie Reynolds, who hired me away as his assistant to help with the dog-faced boy he was promoting. Charlie promised to help me get home."

That last was indeed the truth; then Fedor grew more sober. "But every time I bring it up, Charlie says, 'after the next town, after the next booking.' I'm not sure he ever intends to really take me home."

"We'll just have to insist!" Addie asserted.

"It's worse than that," Fedor looked down. "No one seems to have even heard of Ziymia anymore. It's not on any other maps, so it certainly follows that no one would know how to get there. I myself am not even certain that it wasn't some childish dream…"

"Fedor, you mustn't talk like that," Addie scolded. "We simply *have* to get you home."

Fedor was touched that she felt so strongly; he managed a slight smile and murmured quietly, "I would truly love to show it to you."

"All right then, that's settled," Addie proclaimed. She took a breath and then, with her voice lower but still full of excitement, "Tell me more about your kingdom, Fedor."

And with that simple request began an hours-long conversation allowing Fedor to skillfully interweave reality with its fanciful rival into a tapestry of adventure intended to entertain and delight his new friend. He strove above all else to banish those tears that had marred her face—and had gnawed his own heart—for as long as he could muster the strength and imagination to keep them away. But in doing so, he also had to push away, for now, the awful thoughts of what might happen if she discovered who he really was.

For Fedor himself, Addie meant more to him than being able to cheer a girl up. He had managed to make a friend, a difficult and rare accomplishment in the confined and secluded life he was leading. And he knew he would be leaving this city in a short time. All he could hope for was to leave Addie with some pleasant memories and inspirations to get her through the tough times, that she might think of him on occasion, and that at some future time, they might reunite under better circumstances.

A sharp knock at the prop room door abruptly shattered the reveries of a distant land. "Addie? You in there?" It was Patrick.

Fedor scurried over to hide behind a stack of tables. He whispered back toward Addie, "Charlie wouldn't like it that I've been visiting with you when I should be working. So if anyone asks, you never met me."

Another knock. "Addie?" Patrick poked his head in.

"I'm here, Patrick," she called out, somewhat confused but excited to become a conspirator with Fedor.

"Your father wants me to walk you home for supper."

"Let me get my things together and I'll meet you downstairs."

"Okay, Princess." Patrick left the sanctum and Fedor emerged from his hiding place.

The evening performance would not begin for almost three more hours. Addie grabbed her cane along with a couple of pieces of origami that she'd been working on and prepared to follow Patrick. "I'll be at the show tonight," she noted to Fedor.

"I uh…won't be at tonight's performance," admitted Fedor. "I have to clean Dog-Boy's cage and uh…take care of some things." Then he got inspired, "But if you're backstage, Dog-Boy knows who you are. I'll train him to do a special bark every time he sees you smile."

Amused interest consumed Addie. "I'll be in the stage-left wing." She began to make her way through the maze of props toward the door when she stopped and turned. "Fedor? Can you introduce me to Dog-Boy?"

Fedor had to think. "Come downstairs to the basement dressing rooms after the show tonight. I'll hide Charlie's liquor, and sooner or later, he'll leave the dressing room to go get more. When he leaves, knock on the door, and I'll, uh, introduce you to Dog-Boy."

A short while later Patrick and Addie were strolling the sidewalk towards the Alexander home in the cool of the afternoon. The city noises softened as the two turned down the tree-lined residential street. Though Addie had her hand on Patrick's guiding arm, it was unclear who was leading whom.

"Hey, Kiddo, seems like you've got a little more spring in your step today," Patrick observed.

"I made a new friend today, Patrick."

"Yeah, who?"

"His name is Fedor," Addie announced.

"Huh? Fedor? Where'd you meet him? Who is he?"

"He works for Mr. Reynolds, helps take care of the dog-boy."

Patrick squinted and scratched his head. "Maybe I've missed him. I haven't seen any Fedor lurking about. Are you sure he's not another one of your imaginary friends?"

"Fedor's real, Patrick. He's not much older than me, and he's very smart and very nice," Addie boasted. "And he made me a princess!" She showed Patrick the signet ring.

Patrick took a close look at it and shrugged. "Okay, Princess. Just be sure he doesn't give you any fleas."

Addie suppressed a giggle. "Patrick, be nice!"

"So I got one for ya, Addie. The doctor tells this fellow: 'That pain in your leg is caused by old age.' And the man says, 'But Doc, my other leg is the same age, and *it* doesn't hurt."

Addie snickered. "Oh, Patrick, I don't know why Papa doesn't put you in the show."

"You remember what he said: I've got to make *him* laugh first. But gee whiz, I never saw such a sourpuss!" lamented Patrick.

"Oh, he is not!"

"Oh yeah? The other day I asked him, 'Ezra, have you heard my last joke?' and he said, 'I hope so!'"

Addie laughed again, but then they both turned silent. Addie knew that Patrick couldn't realize how special it was having Fedor as a friend at a time in her life when friends seemed to be at a premium. It was frustrating that Patrick thought Fedor was imaginary—it almost made her wonder if Patrick wasn't right. And it saddened her that Fedor would doubtlessly be leaving in mere days. But she couldn't think about that now.

The increasing fragrance from the Gardenias in the Alexander front yard let Addie know that she and Patrick were nearing home, and they shortly arrived at the front door of her residence.

"Thank you for walking me home, Patrick."

"Anything for you, Princess." The housekeeper opened the door. "Good evening, Mrs. Kump," Patrick waved, turned, and quickly departed as Addie entered the house.

"Good evening, Miss Addie," welcomed Mrs. Kump.

"Mmm, supper smells good," Addie chirped.

Chapter Six

Addie and Ezra sat at opposite ends of the table in their mahogany and stained glass dining room, finishing their soup. Mrs. Kump took away Addie's bowl, replacing it with a laden dinner plate.

"Peas are at three o'clock; potatoes at ten and pork chop at six," Mrs. Kump gently prompted Addie.

"Thank you, Mrs. Kump," Addie replied as Mrs. Kump proceeded to swap out Ezra's dishes as well.

The meal continued silently. Ezra studied a folded newspaper in between bites. The only sound was the ticking of the grandfather clock in the parlor.

Addie broke the silence, "Papa?"

"Yes, Sweetheart." He didn't look up.

"You know the dog-boy in the show?"

"Yes."

"I think Mr. Reynolds is cruel to him."

Ezra looked at her. "What makes you say that?"

"I heard some things."

"Look, Addie," Ezra asserted sternly, "In the first place, it's none of our business. And in the second place, if a fellow *looks* like that, no telling what his *mind* is doing."

"Looks like what, Papa?"

"All…hairy and…Listen, Sweetheart. I've known Charlie Reynolds for a lot of years. He wouldn't do anything like that."

"But Papa…"

"That'll be the end of it now. Eat your supper."

"But…"

Ezra had gone back to his newspaper.

"Yes, Papa." Addie conceded.

A moment later she piped up again. "Papa?"

"Yes?"

"Papa, have you ever thought about getting married again?"

"Sweetheart, what are you talking about?"

"Don't you ever want to have someone else to keep you company besides me?"

"You know your mother was very special to me."

"Yes, I know, but does that mean you have to always be alone?"

"What's all this about, Addie?"

"I mean, it's not like nobody would want you. Even Rachel says she thinks you're handsome."

Ezra swallowed, not knowing how to respond. "Addie, it's unseemly for young girls to try to play matchmaker. I think you'd better let people take care of their own matters while you tend to yours."

She had done what she could, she told herself. At the very least she had planted a seed, and that would have to be satisfying enough for now.

. . .

Reynolds and Fedor were in the middle of their act in that evening's performance. Reynolds stood by with his buggy whip as Fedor went through his routine, launching into a handstand as the music played.

Out of the corner of his eye, Fedor noticed Addie arriving and taking to her stool in the wings. As she did so, he let out a non-ferocious bark, more of an affectionate "yip" than anything else.

Addie began to realize the utterance was aimed at her, and a smile started to grow on her face. This precipitated more of the same kind of bark, fulfilling Fedor's promise. The barking, in turn, caused Addie to grin even more broadly, which led to… more barking.

"Yip, yip, yip, yip, yip!"

Soon, Addie was giggling hysterically to a constant barrage of the strange barks, bringing the performance temporarily to a yipping halt.

The audience, too, was amused by Fedor's odd behavior, and laughter abounded from all quarters—except a furious Reynolds, who seemingly had lost control of his charge. His futile attempts at regaining Fedor's attention while Fedor bounded around the stage on all-fours, stopping periodically to wave his arms and howl, brought humiliating guffaws from the gallery.

Reynolds stormed around the stage, cracking his whip in vain, bringing ever more laughter—and barking—from all around. In his fury, Reynolds attempted to plant himself in front of the energetic Fedor to regain his attention but, in doing so, stumbled over a stage brace, dislodging a large scenic flat that began to teeter.

Fedor caught sight of this, ceasing his outcries immediately as he observed that the careening flat was heading toward an unsuspecting Addie. Panicked, he shouted:

"Look out!"

He dove for Addie, pulling her out of the way as the flat tumbled to the stage with a crash. The music abruptly halted as bits of debris fell into the orchestra pit. Many in the audience rose to their feet with a collective gasp. Then, as the dust began to settle, murmurs started to emanate from the crowd.

"Did you hear that? The bloke spoke English! He ain't no dog-boy!" groused one man to his neighbor, loudly.

"It's a fake! I knew it. Fake!" shouted another.

A horrified Ezra growled at his employees in the wings opposite the mishap, "Victor, bring down the main curtain! Now! Somebody get Miss Linnette back up here." Stagehand Victor heaved on the ropes for all he was worth as another stagehand scampered off to find the dancer.

Once the curtain was down, Ezra himself hurried out into the footlights. "Ladies and gentlemen! Please don't be alarmed. Everyone is all right, and damage is…uh, minimal. We apologize for the slight mishap, but please stay with us as we'd like to continue this evening's entertainment with an encore performance from Miss Joanna Linnette. Maestro, if you please…"

The orchestra members quickly resumed their positions, shuffled their sheet music, and struck up Miss Linnette's intro just as she appeared in the wings, still fastening her last button. On cue, she strutted into the footlights, and the low-brow audience settled back into their seats in perfect accordance with Ezra's hurried calculation.

Behind the main curtain, a group of performers gathered

around Addie as the stagehands restored the scenery to order and set up for the next act. Ezra rushed over toward his daughter.

"Sweetheart, are you injured?"

"I'm fine, Papa," Addie assured as she straightened her dress and hair.

Ezra glanced around the area, "Bridgette! Come here. Get Addie out of here to someplace she'll be safe."

Corseted Bridgette wandered over and took Addie's arm. "Sure thing, Ezra. Come on, Honey." She led Addie towards the rear stage door as Addie wriggled her arm out of Bridgette's grasp.

After confirming that Addie was indeed unscathed, Ezra stormed over to intercept Reynolds, who was gathering his props, as Fedor stood quietly by. But, upon the approach of a fuming Ezra, Fedor stepped back reflexively.

"Charlie, that's it!" Ezra growled furiously. "I'm cutting the run short. I can't have—"

But Reynolds held up his hand. "Look, I'm dreadfully sorry about all this. But don't be foolish, Ezra! When word of this gets around the crowds'll be twice as big. How can you pass up such an opportunity? Everyone and their neighbor will want to see if the 'wild man' will go berserk again."

Charlie always did have a way of taking the wind out of Ezra's sails. "You want berserk? I'll give you berserk!" Ezra threatened.

"Look, Ezra. It won't happen again." Reynolds glared at Fedor. "He just got a little carried away, is all, too many weeks on the road. You know what it's like. What do you say?"

Ezra ran his hand through his hair as he contemplated the situation. Unfortunately, Reynolds was right. The crowds *would* get bigger.

"All right," Ezra conceded. One more performance. But tomorrow night that's it." With that, he stormed off.

Reynolds called after him: "Spoken like a true Solomon, Ezra, my boy!" Reynolds' cheerful expression receded as Ezra disappeared from view.

Bridgette led Addie circuitously to the theatre's lobby which, during the performance, was nearly empty, brightly lit, and even had a few chairs and a settee where Addie could settle. Thus, it seemed to conform to Ezra's instruction about safety.

"Here y'are Honey. You're in the lobby. You should be nice and safe. Stay here, and your papa'll pick you up after the show."

"Bridgette?" asked Addie.

"Yeah, Sweetie?"

"Have you met a fellow that works for Mr. Reynolds named Fedor?"

Bridgette looked puzzled. "Fedor, huh? I dunno, Honey. Not ringin' any bells. Now listen, I gotta go on stage in a minute. You stay here and keep both of us out of trouble, okay?"

Addie hated being talked to like a child. And Bridgette didn't know of Fedor either. Was she going crazy? Had she dreamed it all? For now, she could only settle into her favourite settee near the band organ and ponder all the strange events of the day as the music from the auditorium wafted over her. She would know soon enough if it was all in her imagination.

Below in the basement, Reynolds kicked open the dressing room door and shoved Fedor across the room, where he crashed into the wire cage and landed in a laundry pile. Reynolds looked over the dressing table. Cursing, he picked up the empty liquor bottle he found there and heaved it, shattering it in a corner, causing Fedor to wince and cover his face with his arms.

"Stay in here till I get back!" the red-faced Reynolds fumed, turning to exit, and slamming the door behind him.

Under the stairs, not far away, Addie had been waiting for this moment, though she hadn't expected it to be this soon or this troubling. As Reynolds tromped up the metal stairs, Addie emerged from her hiding place and made her way to the door of dressing room six.

She knocked, whispering. "Fedor?"

Her voice set Fedor's heart racing. He pulled himself upright in a panic and started scrambling to prepare for her. Hands shaking, he put on a pair of cloth gloves and grabbed Charlie's buggy whip. "I'm coming Addie," he called out. When satisfied that he was as prepared as he could be, he nudged open the door to find Addie, who managed a nervous smile.

"Hello, Fedor."

"Addie, come in! We've been waiting for you. Come this way," he guided her by her elbow. "Sit here." He perched her on the dressing table's chair which he had turned to face into the room.

He then used the buggy whip to reach across the room behind Addie and rattle it against the metal cage, making sounds to simulate an excited creature inside. "Yes, boy. Yes. She's here. Calm down now," Fedor instructed his invisible roommate.

"Is he tame?" Addie asked, fidgeting in expectation.

"Oh yes, he wouldn't hurt anyone," Fedor continued, rattling the cage. He then shifted his body closer to the cage so the canine whimpering sounds he made would sound as if they came from the cage's occupant. "He remembers you," he said, shifting his body back.

"Why do you keep him in a cage?"

"Mostly for show…you know…ballyhoo. But also for his own protection. We never quite know what he'll get into. Uh…I heard about the troubles in the act this evening."

"It was actually kind of fun. Mr. Reynolds didn't exactly appreciate it, though," Addie grinned.

Immediately, the dog-boy responded as he had on stage. "Yip, yip, yip, yip, yip!" causing Addie to laugh melodiously.

Fedor shifted position to make his voice come from a different place and attempted to calm his alter ego. "Now, boy, that's enough. Time to be quiet now. Shhh."

Then he turned to Addie. "Miss Addie, I wanted to thank you."

"Thank me? For what?" she blushed.

"Yesterday I saw you when you were sad. You were feeling alone—that you were the only one who would ever know how you were feeling because you're different from most people. Isn't that right?"

"Yes…yes, that's right! How did you know?"

"Because that's the same feeling I have inside me…" Fedor had to be careful; he didn't want her to have to deal with exactly *how* he was different. "You've freed me, Miss Addie! Your…blindness is a special gift that lets you see me more clearly than anyone ever has. You have no idea what it means to—"

"—to have someone else who understands?" Addie interrupted. "Yes, as a matter of fact, I think I do."

There was a pause. Fedor's heart leapt upon hearing that she felt the same things he did. Then he grabbed the buggy whip again and started making noises at the cage. "It's okay, boy. Shhh."

"Can I pet him?" Addie asked, swallowing nervously.

Fedor had to think, "All right, just a moment." He stepped over to the cage and noisily undid the latch. "There, come on out, boy." He opened the gate so it could creak. Then he got closer to Addie and got down on his knees. "Give me your hand, Addie."

She held her hand out tentatively, trembling with anticipation.

Fedor then took her hand and placed it on his own face.

The touch immediately calmed her. She gently stroked his head and face. "Mmm…he's soft…"

Fedor's eyes moistened at the gentle touch of another human being. He hadn't experienced the joy of such a tender connection since infancy.

Suddenly, there was a harsh knock at the door. But, with no patience for a response, the door immediately swung open, and Ezra stepped through. "Charlie, I just wanted to—"

A surprised Ezra then saw Addie and Fedor huddled closely, and a look of horror came over him. "Get away from her, you brute!" He rushed over and shoved Fedor away.

"But Papa! He's not—"

"Addie, leave here this instant!" Ezra fumed. "Go upstairs to my office and wait."

"But Papa…" Addie's fists clenched.

"I said go…NOW!" Ezra was in no mood to be argued with, and a palpably frustrated Addie tearfully rose, trembling, to depart.

Fedor sputtered, "Please, sir, you don't understand."

"I understand all too well. Where's Charlie?"

Reynolds' slurred voice boomed from the corridor. "Do I

hear someone mention my name?" Reynolds entered, a partially-full bottle in one hand. He almost collided with Addie as she exited.

His breath repulsed Ezra, "I came down here to reconsider and offer to let you stay a couple more days, Charlie. Looks like I came at just the right time. Your…your…*whatever-he-is* had his paws all over Addie!"

Charlie couldn't believe it, "Ezra, you must be joking. The boy would never…"

"Look, Charlie, I've got advertising space booked, so unfortunately, you're still on tomorrow night. After that, you'd better be on the first train. And in the meantime, keep that…*creature* locked up! I don't want him—or *you*—anywhere near my daughter again."

Ezra stormed out, leaving Reynolds and Fedor warily eyeing each other.

Chapter Seven

The next morning, Addie had a large braille book spread out on the desk in the study of the Alexander home and was half-heartedly poring over it with her fingers. She was still smarting from the scene her father had caused with Fedor last night, completely baffled by Papa's anger and intractability. She knew Fedor didn't do anything to deserve such treatment, and she hadn't disobeyed anyone. So the events, as she recalled them, were a mystery.

Rachel appeared at the open French doors, carrying two more of the imposing braille books in her arms. She knocked politely on the door frame.

"Good morning, Addie! I got some new books for today's lessons…What're you reading?"

Addie continued moving her fingers over the raised dots. "Oh, um…The story of how Jesus healed a blind beggar man. I just read that afterwards, he told the man not to tell anyone! Why do you suppose he did that, Rache?"

Rachel put the books down on a nearby table. "Well…I think that it was because if word got around about him doing miracles, his enemies might have seized him before his ministry was complete."

"So God had a plan and a schedule all worked out?"

"Uh-huh. Same for all of us." Rachel smiled.

"Does He have a plan for Fedor?" asked Addie.

"I'm sure He does…but who's Fedor?"

"A boy with the show. He has some terrible problems, and the Dog-Boy as well…"

"Dog-Boy?" exclaimed a puzzled Rachel.

"But Fedor's so kind," Addie continued. "Rachel, why does God let bad things happen to people like him?"

Rachel paused. This, of course, was one of the deepest questions facing all humans. Could she answer it well enough for Addie? "A lot of folks ask that question, Addie. They think trials and misfortunes are one of the most confusing things about life. But I think they help us to understand our lives better."

Addie skewed her mouth skeptically, "How?"

"Well, if there were no such thing as sadness, how would you know happiness when it came along? Or beauty…How could we appreciate something beautiful if nothing was plain or distasteful…or ugly?"

"It still doesn't seem fair."

Rachel opened a satchel of books and began shuffling papers. "No, I suppose not. Life sometimes isn't fair…like right now when we have to begin our lessons. We've got a lot to cover in the few sessions we have left, you and I."

"Do we have to study just now?" Addie pleaded. "Couldn't we go on another picnic?"

Rachel shook her head. "Otta, Wanna, and Godda."

"What?" puzzled Addie.

"Those are the three hungry creatures that gobble up our time —Otta, the things we '*ought*' to do, like wash the dishes or brush our teeth; Wanna, the things we '*want*' to do, like go for a picnic or listen to music, and Godda, the things we *have got* to do, like eat so that we can live, or work so that we can pay our debts. Otta, Wanna, and Godda. They're always competing for our time, and we have to live our lives choosing which one will control us at any given moment to help us best get through the day. It seems like Wanna is tugging on you right now for a picnic."

"Well, yes," admitted Addie, trying to stay hopeful.

"But you remember the story of what happened to old Jonah when he didn't do what he was supposed to do?"

Addie lowered her head a bit, "The sailors threw him overboard and he got swallowed by a great fish."

"That's right." Rachel smiled. "Fortunately we're not in a boat right now. But *un*fortunately, Godda is breathing down our necks to get our schoolwork done. Did you finish your arithmetic?"

"Yes'm," replied a disappointed Addie.

She felt her way over to a shelf, where she took down her mathematics book and removed her braille assignment sheet. As she handed it to Rachel, Ezra appeared at the open door, holding a brochure in his hand. "Excuse me, ladies, but I have some good news."

Addie was glad for the distraction. Ezra strolled over near her. "Addie, how would you like to attend a school with others just like yourself?"

"You mean other blind children?"

"That's right," Ezra continued. "But they say the emphasis is on education, not blindness."

Rachel perked up. "It sounds promising, Ezra!"

Ezra handed the brochure and letter to Rachel. He knew he was not up to the task of continuing his daughter's education himself. And, of course, he had other responsibilities. So, a school specifically for blind students seemed like an ideal solution for the challenges Rachel's departure would cause.

"What's it called?" asked Addie, somewhat skeptical as she shifted in her chair.

"It's the Mary Helen Mattison Academy. It's over in Sheffield," explained Ezra.

Rachel was less enthused. "Ezra, it's a boarding school."

"And Addie'll be with lots of other girls her own age." Now defensive, Ezra turned to Addie, "It'll do you a world of good, Sweetheart."

Suddenly, it didn't seem so wonderful to Addie. "You're sending me *away*? You mean I couldn't live here with you anymore, Papa?"

"Oh, it's not as bad as all that, Sweetheart. We'll still see each other…at least once every few weeks." Ezra began to see on both their faces that his words were not helping.

Addie was overwhelmed with emotion and dread. She had been privately taught all her life. It had made her feel special and had allowed her to excel. Perhaps the school would be a good option, maybe even a great one. But the changes were coming too quickly for her to absorb. She had always believed her father loved her, but now even that was in doubt.

"Everyone just wants to be rid of me!" she sobbed. "Even God must hate me!"

She rushed out of the room and up the stairs, headed for her room.

Ezra called after her, "Wait, Sweetheart. I didn't mean…" Exasperated, he let her go, turning to Rachel, "It'd be the best thing for her. I should think she'd be grateful. What do I *do*, Rachel?"

Rachel sympathetically took his hand. "Just keep loving her with all your might, Ezra. Whatever you do will be right if that's what's in your heart."

Ezra looked into her kind gaze. Over the years, Rachel had become more than Addie's teacher. She was much more like family. What he saw now was someone he would come to miss as much as Addie would, maybe more. Rachel was a solid foundation in both Addie's life and Ezra's. She could always be depended on to do the right thing with a gentle and joyful spirit, and her counsel, when needed, was always correct. She had both an inner beauty and outer calm that Ezra wasn't sure he was ready to part with any more than Addie was.

After school, Rachel dropped Addie off at the Ruby Palace Theatre. Once inside, using her cane, Addie quickly descended the stairs to the basement dressing rooms. The murmur of multiple conversations and occasional laughter let her know the corridor was not empty. She counted her steps from the last stair and soon came to the door of Fedor's dressing room. She knocked.

"You may enter," came the response. She was relieved that it was Fedor's voice. She opened the door, and Fedor put down the book he was reading.

"Addie!" he spoke in a loud, whispered tone. "You're not supposed to be here! What if your father…?"

"I had to say thank you—for introducing me to Dog-Boy. Is he still here?" Addie straightened her dress nervously.

"Yes, but um…" began Fedor, "He's asleep."

"Oh, I'm sorry," she whispered, wincing. There was a moment of uncertain silence. "And I also wanted to say…I'm sorry for the way Papa acted last night."

Fedor managed a brave smile. "That's why we have our dreams, you and I, to get us through the sad times."

She smiled tentatively.

"But, listen, Addie—Charlie is going to be back soon. It would not be good for him to find you here."

"I…just wanted to talk and tell you those things," she said as she nervously fingered the tip of her cane.

"Can we go to your thinking place to talk, then?" offered Fedor.

"Patrick might find us there," she cautioned. Then a thought occurred: "I know! There's another place they wouldn't find us. This way." She stepped toward the door but turned back. "Will Dog-Boy be all right?"

"Yes, he'll be fine. He needs his rest."

Addie extended her hand to lead him. But Fedor knew he couldn't let her touch his hairy hands. "One moment," he urged as he turned to reach for his gloves, quickly putting them on and then catching up to take her hand.

"Ooh, gloves," she said, "Are you cold?"

"It's a little chilly here in the basement." Fedor died a little inside every time he engaged in another deception, no matter how small. Addie deserved better, he thought.

. . .

Addie led him toward the rear of the building, where the basement corridor took a sharp turn and became rather darker, for it was unused. Not long after the turn was a door, which Addie found by rapping the wall with her cane until she heard a hollow sound.

"Here it is," she proclaimed with a proud smile.

Fedor knew only that he was standing in a dim area, but he was intrigued. He opened the door and peered inside—it was utter blackness.

"Hmm, kind of dark," he remarked as he glanced around the wall near the door. There, he found a portable lantern hanging on the wall, with a small tin of matches attached next to it.

"Ah, here we are," he said, taking a match, striking it, and lighting the lantern. "Casting light into the darkness."

"Sorry, I didn't know," admitted Addie sheepishly.

Fedor removed the lantern from its hook and thrust it into the void. What was revealed was a fairly large, dusty space, apparently used for storage like Addie's thinking spot, but even more utilitarian and forgotten.

Fedor took Addie's hand, and the two of them stepped into the gloomy expanse, closing the door behind them. The lantern moved the shadows of unknown forms around them as they began to explore. Rows of obsolete and broken theatre seats, dusty wooden boxes, and various theatre paraphernalia were scattered haphazardly. But the space was largely empty.

"We're right below the stage," Addie explained.

Fedor looked up and saw small slivers of light in a rectangle that revealed a trap door leading to the performing area, useful, he knew, for many things in a theatre.

"Miss Addie, a princess like you doesn't belong in a kingdom of the underworld," mused Fedor, as he continued to peer around the darkness. They neared an old upright rehearsal piano, missing several keys. "One of these days you shall have music and dancing in your kingdom." He pressed the keys to strike a glorious chord, but the ancient instrument's lack of tuning rendered only dissonance. He immediately backed off. "Ooh. Sorry."

As the piano's mournful tones faded, silence ensued for a moment.

"You know your Papa would not be happy if he saw us right now," Fedor said as he continued to thrust the lantern into the shadows.

Addie sighed. "I don't care. This morning he said he wanted to send me off to a boarding school. Not only am I losing Rachel, but I couldn't even be with Papa anymore."

Fedor pulled up a small empty nail keg, dusted it off for Addie. "Here, you can sit on this throne, Your Highness."

Addie felt it and took a seat. "Thanks."

"Now, Miss Addie that school sounds to me like it could be a grand new adventure. Your papa must want what's best for you. It'd be a big new world to explore. You know you can't spend your life hiding in dusty basements."

"I know," Addie lowered her head. "It's just another piece of growing up that frightens me."

Fedor stooped to pick up a discarded wall clock. "I understand completely," he agreed. He pried open the clock to examine its dusty mechanism. "Growing up seems like it can't come quickly enough—until it's upon us. Sometimes, I'd just like to shrink down to the size of an ant and walk around inside things like this clock, watching its springs and gears, away from the world's cares. Or maybe I could grow huge and look down on the world the way it looks down on us sometimes." Fedor sighed, and quiet flooded in for a moment.

"I've never known a friend like you, Fedor," Addie said with a sense of sad admiration. A few more moments of silence passed until a rustling sound broke the stillness from a corner across from them.

"What's that?" Addie whispered.

Fedor raised the lantern to illuminate the area. "Just a rat," he said and sat down near her on another keg.

"Ooh!" Addie shuddered. She didn't know exactly what a rat might look like, but she knew Rachel hated them.

"It's all right. He's afraid of us." Fedor shrugged, then reflected softly, "There have been times when it seemed like rats were my best company."

"Back when you worked for the fairs?"

"Uh-huh." Fedor realized he was getting a bit gloomy, when Addie needed his support. "But even when Charlie's cross," he heartened, "It's so much better these days. I get to work in a show, see all sorts of countries and cities…and even meet the crowned princess of Ziymia!"

Addie blushed and gave an embarrassed little laugh.

Suddenly, Fedor's eye was caught by a larger dark mass near the wall, not far away. "What's this?" He picked up the lantern and walked over to it.

"Addie!" His voice was filled with excitement. "It's an old ticket booth!" And indeed it was.

Addie grabbed her cane and made her way toward Fedor's voice. "I think I remember it when I was little. It came from another old theatre I think. Papa eventually changed things around so that the ticket window is now part of the main building."

Though the years had abused it, Fedor could tell that the booth had once been glorious. Rococo filigree embellished its base, with more on its crown. The decorations were covered with flaking layers of gold paint but its grand past still shone through the dust and decay. The central section was a rusted metal cage made of elaborate wrought iron with openings only big enough to speak and pass tickets through.

"It's beautiful, Addie; or at least it was once," Fedor narrated as he walked around the relic. "There's a door in the back. Let me try it." After a bit of rattling and squeaking, it opened and Fedor entered the booth.

"Be careful!" cautioned Addie.

"Don't you worry, Miss. This booth is just about ready for business," Fedor said wryly—something about being behind that wrought iron brought out the entertainer in him.

"Fedor what…?" Addie stammered.

"Hurry, hurry, hurry!" Fedor barked. "See the incredible Dog-Boy and the exotic and lovely Princess Addie of far-away Ziymia in the adventure of a lifetime. Thrills, laughs, amazement! All this can be yours my friends for the incredible admission price of a mere two smiles and a giggle. Hurry! Hurry! Hurry!"

Addie applauded and chuckled merrily.

"And you, young woman, how many tickets would you require?"

"I, um…"

"I understand by your smiles and giggles that you intend to acquire enough tickets for your entire family and all your neighbors!"

Addie continued her laughter until tears welled up in her eyes.

"Be advised that those tears, young woman, the tears of laughter, are the only ones allowed on these premises. Hurry, hurry, hurry!"

Fedor paused his spiel and just gazed in wonder at Addie, smiling and laughing; the most beautiful sight he had seen in all his years. It was something he never wanted to end. And yet he knew it must—and sooner than he would like.

As her laughing subsided Addie had a request: "Fedor, tell me another story about Ziymia."

"Well, Miss Addie, for one thing I need to get back to Dog-Boy. It's nearly his feeding time. For another thing you need to experience Ziymia for yourself. It's just about the most…"

Fedor had attempted to open the door to the booth and the latch was not budging. "Just a minute…" He rattled it and tried to turn the knob again. Nothing happened. "Addie, it won't open," he admitted. He tried banging on it to shake something loose. Nothing. He was a prisoner in this miniature jail.

"Oh no! Can't you get out?" cried Addie.

"I'm afraid I'm incarcerated."

"Are you sure? Try it again."

Fedor continued rattling the knob, turning it and banging on the latch. Addie came around the back to see if she could find a secondary latch or turn the knob from the outside. She couldn't make it open either. "What do we do?" she pleaded.

"I think you're going to have to go for help," sighed Fedor.

"All right, but who?"

"Anyone with tools. A stagehand, your friend Patrick, even Charlie if you have to."

Addie grabbed her cane and determinedly started for the door. "Don't you worry, Fedor. I'll get help, for certain."

Fedor watched her go with much sadness in his heart.

Several minutes later, Patrick, toolbox in hand was a pace behind Addie as she steadfastly marched along the basement corridor.

"I can't wait to finally meet this Fedor mate of yours. How did he get locked in there?" a breathless Patrick asked, trying to lug the heavy toolbox and still keep up with a scurrying Addie.

"He was entertaining me. And all of a sudden, he couldn't get out," she explained.

They turned the corner and came to the door beneath the stage. "We'll take care of it," assured Patrick. The lantern was not in its customary wall hook, so Patrick opened the door. Sure enough, there was the glowing lantern, some yards away, sitting on the transaction shelf of the old ticket booth.

"Fedor? I brought help," Addie called out.

No answer.

"Fedor, I've come to get you out," exclaimed Patrick as he and Addie approached the booth. As they arrived, Patrick walked around it and peered inside. "There's nobody here, Addie."

"Fedor!" Addie called again.

Patrick tried the door in the rear of the booth, opening and closing, latching and unlatching several times. "Nothing wrong with the door hitch either."

Addie was mystified. "I…don't know what could've happened. He was here!"

Patrick put the toolbox down and faced Addie, arms folded. "Now, Addie," he said as sternly as he could muster. "You're too old now for imaginary friends; and if this is some kind of a joke, it's not funny."

"No, Patrick! He was here! I don't know where he could've gone. I'm so sorry if I took you away from your work." Addie was feeling disturbed enough, and the fact that she had wasted Patrick's time didn't make her feel any better.

Patrick could see she was upset. "Well, all right, Princess." He stooped to pick up his toolbox. "I have to get back to work. I hope you find him." He grabbed the lantern. "You comin'?"

Addie reluctantly followed him back out to the corridor.

Chapter Eight

I t was about two in the afternoon. The marquee for The Ruby Palace Theatre contained a seven-foot glass case with a roster of all the acts currently playing. Fourth on the list was "Charles Reynolds Presents the Dog-Faced Boy." A stagehand opened the case to place a smaller sign above this listing: "Tonight! FINAL PERFORMANCE." Two passersby, a man and a woman, observed this activity from the sidewalk, looked at each other, and immediately stepped toward the box office window to purchase tickets.

Meanwhile, Patrick arrived at his station in the limelight booth to prep the equipment for the evening's performance. As he entered the room and brought up the gaslight, he noticed something new on the stool Addie usually inhabited. It was a small package wrapped in white paper, with an envelope addressed to Addie Alexander. This immediately piqued Patrick's curiosity. Now, he had to get this to her to find out what it was all about. He also knew there was one place she was likely to be.

Addie had cried herself to sleep in her usual spot on the velvet throne, tightly clutching a stuffed toy turtle in the silent, musty prop room. Patrick stepped into the space and approached his unhappy friend. Despite the dried tear stains, she was an elegantly pretty little girl in the peace of sleep. It seemed an unfortunate imposition to wake her, but he had his mission. He jostled her arm.

"Psst. Hey Addie. Wake up. I've got somethin' for ya."

Addie stirred, "Wha'? Who's there?"

"It's me, Patrick."

"Mmm…Patrick? What is it?" She was coming around but still not quite conscious.

"Somebody left this for you on your stool in the booth."

Addie sat up, and Patrick handed her the package. She examined the package with her fingers and discovered the envelope. "It's either a note or a card I think. Patrick, could you read it to me?" She held out the envelope to him.

"Thought you'd never ask." He opened it and read:

My dearest Miss Addie,

I am so sorry for the deception at the ticket booth. I couldn't bring myself to say goodbye to you. Please accept this gift. Perhaps someday we can pick them from the trees together. Thank you for your friendship. I'll never forget you.

Love, Fedor.

"Well, I'll be flummoxed. He's not imaginary after all!" admitted Patrick.

Addie opened the package—while Patrick was reading—to discover that the white-paper wrapping covered a container of small, sugary, round objects… "Gumdrops!" she exclaimed.

"Wait, there's more," noted Patrick.

P.S. We shall be leaving on the late train to-night.

Addie frowned. "Oh, Patrick, he writes as if he's already left, and I didn't even get to tell him goodbye!" Tears began to flow again. "I *have* to tell him goodbye!"

"Well, wait a minute there, Princess. Your Papa gave strict orders. You're not even s'posed to catch the show tonight."

"Oh, what does Papa care?" She clutched her turtle.

"Addie, he's your father. You have to listen to him."

But the tearful Addie was starting to scheme, "Listen. I have an idea. I'll need your help, Patrick. Can I count on you?"

"I…I don't know, Princess—Your Pa's my boss."

She waved his objection away, "He'll never even know. And it would mean so much to me…and Fedor. Patrick?"

Patrick was ill at ease with this. He paced a bit and stroked his chin. Then he turned back to Addie, sighing. "What's your plan, Princess?"

Addie stood and hugged him, smiling. Some of the plan was still coming to her, so she started thinking aloud, "Well, they're leaving on the late train. That's the ten o'clock, right?"

"Aye."

"And the show gets over when, nine-thirty or so?"

"Well, yes, but your fellows'll be packed and on their way to the station as soon as their act is done." Patrick pointed out.

"That's true. But *you* won't be free until the show is over. And you're the key part of this…So the show lets out about nine-thirty. And Papa usually stays in his office till about midnight. Even later, sometimes."

"What're you gettin' at?" Patrick demanded.

"Don't you see, Patrick? After the show lets out, you'd have just enough time to hitch up the wagon and take me from our house to the train station so I could say goodbye to Fedor. I could be back home and in bed, and you'd be safe before Papa ever left his office." Perhaps Fedor had inspired her to be a bit more conspiratorial. But it was for a good cause, she told herself.

"What about your housekeeper, Mrs. Kump?" Patrick asked.

Addie scowled. But then she perked up again as she realized, "It's her night off!"

Patrick rubbed his eyebrows. "Hmm…it *sounds* like it ought to work."

"Then you'll do it for us, Patrick?!"

Patrick offered a hesitant grin, "Well, seein' as it's you…" Somehow, he could never deny Addie anything, even at his own peril. She was the little sister he never had.

"Oh, Patrick, you're wonderful! You'll never know how much this means to me."

Patrick started getting into the spirit of conspiracy, "I'll get Lulu hitched up during the intermission, so we'll be all set when the show lets out. I'll come knockin' at your door about nine forty-five. If you're ready to go, we ought to just make it."

"Don't worry. I'll be ready."

. . .

Midway through the evening's performance, Patrick centred his spotlight on an Irish tenor as the singer churned out a heartfelt rendition of "Danny Boy." The song ended to polite applause; the curtain came down, and Bridgette strutted over to change the card to one reading: "The Bavarian Bell Choir." While she did this, a dozen lederhösen-and-dirndl-clad men and women, carrying various-sized handbells, took their positions on stage. Patrick quickly checked his watch as the curtain rose and the bell ringers began their piece. This was the last act before inter-mission.

Addie, meanwhile, sat in near-darkness on a loveseat near the big grandfather clock in the parlor of the Alexander home. The clock's ticking was both soothing and disquieting. Addie clutched her stuffed turtle, listening intently, keeping a vigil for Patrick's eventual knock at the front door.

The clock struck eight times. So far, all was well. Addie pondered what was about to happen: a mad dash to the train station just to say a fond goodbye to a newfound friend she may never hear from again. In a few months, would he remember her? Would she remember him? Fedor had shown himself to be someone with whom she could truly share things, even her thoughts, knowing he had those thoughts too. People like him were rare in Addie's world. She rehearsed over and over what she would say to Fedor when they met for perhaps the last time. As sad as they were, these rambling thoughts still managed to crowd out—at least for now—the other struggles and emotions she would soon face with Rachel's departure.

. . .

As soon as the curtain came down on the Bavarian Bell Choir, Patrick immediately shuttered his spotlight, shut the gas down, and hurried out of the booth to the rear stage door. He ran to the stable next door, grabbed a harness, and started prepping Ezra's horse, Lulu. "Here you go, Lulu, old gal. We're doin' a favour for the princess tonight. Just make sure you don't tell Ezra, huh? That's a girl." He got her hitched to the wagon, gave her some oats, then secured her reins to a nearby post. "I'll be back after the show, old girl." Then he whispered in her ear, "Remember, not a word to Ezra." All was set for immediate action when the show ended. Patrick examined everything one more time. Satisfied, he dashed back into the theatre and hustled to resume his post in the booth.

A few blocks away, Addie maintained her vigil. The clock struck eight-thirty. To Addie's dismay, her eyelids were beginning to get heavy.

Reynolds and Fedor were finishing up their act for the evening: after balancing a ball on his nose, Fedor did his handspring over the bar of flames, landing on the platform without a hitch.

The satisfied look on Ezra's face, as he looked on from the wings, bore witness that the performance had been blessedly uneventful. With a fanfare from the orchestra, the curtain closed to enthusiastic applause from the crowd.

As Charlie and Fedor exited the stage, Ezra met them with a handshake. "Well done, Charlie."

Reynolds smiled weakly. "See now Ezra I told you everything would be fine. And it looks like we had another full house." Fedor stood quietly behind him.

Ezra handed Charlie an envelope. "Yes, very nice. Here's your check, Charlie. Good luck on your next stop." Then he had a benevolent, albeit defensive, thought: "Listen, Charlie. Have your stuff packed and on the loading dock, and when the show's over, I'll have my man take you to the train station in our wagon."

Reynolds held up his hand, "That won't be necessary, Ezra; we can get a cab."

"No, I want to do it, Charlie. Be at the loading dock at nine-thirty. Take care of yourself, huh?"

Ezra headed up to his office.

On the Ruby Palace stage, a barbershop quartet belted out the refrain of "Good Night Ladies" as four dancing girls performed around them. With a final rousing chord, the quartet struck an appropriate tableau for this, the closing act of the evening's performance.

The curtain came down and then immediately rose again for curtain calls. The orchestra splashed out play-off music as the performers rushed on and off for a quick bow. When the curtain came down for a final time, the orchestra had blared its final chord, and the limelight was finally dowsed Patrick looked at his watch. It read nine thirty-one. Starting to panic, he quickly shut down his instrument, stowed the cables, and went to dash out the booth's door, only to be met by Ezra coming the other way. Patrick halted in his tracks.

"Patrick, I've got a job for you," Ezra said matter-of-factly.

"Uh…sure. Whatcha got, Guv?" Patrick was starting to sweat.

"I want you to hitch up the wagon and make sure Mr. Reynolds and his companion get to the station in time for the ten o'clock train. Can I trust you with that?"

"Uh, look, Ezra, I…" Patrick was in torment.

"Is there a problem?" Ezra was firm.

"Er, no, Ezra. No problem. I'll get 'em there."

"They'll need help with their luggage, so I suggest you get moving. You can meet them at the loading dock."

"Yes sir."

Ezra strode off, but Patrick sprinted for the loading dock. He was hoping, praying, that he could load up Reynolds and company and still make a detour to pick up Addie on the way to the station. It was his only chance to make this right still.

Arriving at the dock, Patrick found Reynolds and Fedor waiting and addressed them, "Addie said there was another fellow with you, a bloke named Fedor…"

"I am Fedor," asserted Fedor.

"Oh, uh—all right," said Patrick, scratching his head. But there was no time to lose, and he swiftly began lifting bags into the rig.

After the big trunk, the cage, and all their other gear were loaded into the open-bed wagon, Patrick rechecked his watch: nine forty-one. His heart sank as he knew now that his only chance to even get the gentlemen to their train on time was to drive Lulu directly to the train station as quickly as the poor horse could go—no detour to pick up Addie would be possible.

"Get aboard, gentlemen. We have to go." Patrick urged as he took up the reins. Charlie joined him on the seat while Fedor clambered into the back of the wagon with the gear. With a loud "hyaaa!" they were off.

Only a short time later, Addie was sound asleep, lulled into slumber by the gentle ticking of the great clock. But now the clock erupted to life, moaning out its chimes of doom…ten of them, jolting Addie to wakefulness and causing her to sit up with a start, counting. The final toll of the clock's ten chimes was accompanied by the distant mournful blast of a train whistle.

Addie was heartbroken, "Patrick…the train! Oh no! Fedor!" Her heart pounding, Addie quickly put on her coat, grabbed her cane, and rushed out the front door, not even knowing what possible outcome she could achieve.

Tears began streaming from her eyes as she moved quickly down the street toward the edge of town. "Fedor…" she lamented. Though she still struggled to banish the cobwebs of sleep from her brain, her blood was rushing at the sense of impending loss. How could Patrick have betrayed her so?

Though gas streetlights illuminated the way, the thoroughfare was still rather dimly lit. As a result, when Addie passed through a shadow, a rapidly moving horse and wagon nearly ran her down: Patrick and Lulu had sped past her, coming the other way, unaware of the near collision. Though startled by the noisy rush of the passing wagon, Addie's resolve to get to the train station only intensified. Even if the train had left--and trains were often late, she told herself—she could perhaps get on the next train. And if she could only surprise Fedor, she figured, perhaps it would be a reason for him to remember her. In any event, time was of the essence, and this was one time her blindness frustrated her.

. . .

Patrick pulled up in front of the Alexander home, jumped down, and rushed to the front door. "Addie…I'm sorry…" he called out. He knocked on the unlatched door, which swung open before him; Patrick entered the darkened house. "Addie?…Your pa threw a wrench in the works…Addie?"

He ran up the stairs to her room…no one there. He rushed back down two steps at a time and checked the umbrella stand. "No cane…she must've…Oh my goodness!" Panicked, he dashed back outside. Realizing what must have happened, Patrick climbed back in the wagon and set off to look for Addie.

The lights of the city were mostly behind Addie as she steadfastly continued her lone quest to find Fedor. The tears on her cheeks were dry now, but the wind was kicking up, and flickers of lightning were beginning to appear on the horizon.

On another part of the road, Patrick mumbled to himself between calls for Addie. He held up a lantern, peering off into the dense darkness of the road ahead as he left the streetlights behind. "ADDIE! Boy, is Ezra gonna burn my tail when he--ADDIE!… finds out about…"

Suddenly, he spotted a dim figure off in the far reaches of the lantern's light. "Wait a minute…giddap Lulu." Thunder began to rumble across the sky, and as Patrick pulled up beside the dark, diminutive figure, a flash of lightning revealed that it was indeed Addie.

"Addie! Hey, listen, Kiddo; I'm awful sorry about the train

thing, but your pa kind of…Addie, what're you doing way out here?"

"Leave me alone, Patrick. I'm going to find Fedor."

"In the dark?"

She stopped briefly, not believing he had actually said that. "Dark doesn't make any difference to me, Patrick." She continued down the road; Patrick followed alongside with Lulu and the wagon.

"I suppose it doesn't," he admitted. "But, but there's a storm blowin' up here. You could catch your death. What's your pa gonna say?"

Addie continued straight ahead, undaunted. "He doesn't care. He wants to be rid of me anyway."

"Addie, Addie, come on now. How're you ever going to find this Fedor fellow anyway? His train's miles from here by now." Patrick grew tense as he struggled to understand the emotions of a young girl, a girl he not only cared about but whose safety would be foremost in the mind of his less-than-understanding employer.

"I'll find him." She didn't break her stride.

Patrick was getting flustered. "Addie, you're…you're being silly now. Come on and get in the wagon, and I'll take you on home to your pa."

She ignored him.

"Addie!…ADDIE!" He was getting nowhere. Patrick pulled up on the reins and stopped the wagon. He jumped down and approached Addie on foot. He took her hand, pulling her toward the wagon. "Come on now. I can't let you…"

Addie was starting to get frantic again, "Leave me alone, Patrick! I know what I'm doing." She pulled her hand away and kept walking. Thunder again echoed across the sky.

Even more determined, Patrick grabbed her forcefully and started to move toward the wagon. She squirmed.

"Patrick, don't!"

"I'm sorry, Kiddo, but I can't let you do this to yourself." He struggled with the emotional girl until she finally resorted to using her cane as a weapon: She struck Patrick on the head with it, breaking the cane in two. The blow stunned Patrick long enough for Addie to break free and run. She headed into the thick trees that lined the road, running with all her might. But with her cane of no use and the landscape becoming more rugged, she stumbled frequently, leading to frustration and more tears.

The rising wind now made those tears bitterly cold on her face. Addie was beyond the point of even being able to reason clearly. She began to admit to herself she would never make it to the train station. But if she could just get away from Patrick and take a moment to think…

Patrick chased after her into the woods, but she had a significant lead on him. As the fearful darkness only intermittently receded from the ever-increasing stabs of lightning, his progress was slow. "Addie!" he panted, "Please…ADDIE!"

Addie continued running, reasoning far behind her now. "Fedor!" she cried in vain.

Suddenly she tripped…but there was no ground to meet her! Addie plunged over an embankment, tumbling helplessly into the blackness. A lightning bolt flashed as she fell, screaming and flailing, into the chilled abyss of night. Thunder echoed into silence.

Chapter Nine

The locomotive pulling the night train to Manchester chuffed slowly across the English countryside. Fedor and Charlie, though nestled in their private compartment, had the choice of sweltering in the heat of a car that had been in the sun all day or breathing the coal soot and embers that would engulf them if the windows were to open. As a result of choosing the heat, both of them had nodded off to sleep, in their seats on opposite sides of the compartment, after a long and difficult day.

Suddenly, Fedor awoke with a start and a cry, gasping as he came to grips with consciousness, his throat full of panic. The outburst awakened Charlie as well. It was a side of Fedor that Charlie had not seen before, and he realized that something was wrong. "What is it, Lad? What's happened?"

"Charlie, I just had—I feel something's happened to Addie," he cried, gazing off into the distance.

Charlie peered at him intensely. This seemed serious. "Ezra's girl? What makes you say that, Lad? Why were you dreaming about her?"

"I just saw her falling. Falling into a darkness."

Charlie tried to dismiss it. "I'm sure it was just a dream, Lad. Try to go back to sleep."

"I got to know her, Charlie. We became friends. She's a special person," Fedor admitted, sharing more of himself than he normally would with Charlie.

"Aye," Charlie nodded, "a special person who got our run cut short."

"I know, Charlie," Fedor pleaded. "But this is important. I'm scared that something terrible has happened to her. How can we check on her, Charlie? I want to know if she's all right."

Charlie saw how moved the boy was and considered the options. Maybe expressing concern would even get him back into Ezra's good graces. "Listen, Lad, we've got several days without bookings, so we can take things a bit easy. Our next performance is Saturday in Manchester—The Prince's Theatre. Until then, we can check into the hotel, and tomorrow morning, I'll send Ezra a telegram and we can find out if she's all right. Now go back to sleep."

Fedor was still trying to recover from his feeling of dread. He nodded. "Thank you, Charlie." He closed his eyes, folded his arms, and settled in for the journey.

The following morning Addie awakened slowly as the sun warmed her face. Its brilliance hurt her eyes…

Her *eyes*?!

Yes! Addie opened them to discover that the miracle of sight had come upon her. She gasped, blinking her eyes over and over to ensure that the world she was now seeing would not suddenly vanish.

"I…I can see?" she asked herself as she sat up. "I can *see!*" She basked in the wonder of it, examining her hands, her feet, and the world about her.

But that world was like no environment that other sighted people had ever experienced. It was solid enough. But everything would be judged strange in colour if seeing observers were to examine it. However, Addie had never known colour, so she thought nothing of it.

The rocks, grass, trees, and a gently flowing nearby stream would be recognizable to us, but their forms were quirky, with unexpected textures and simplified shapes.

The tops of the trees were truncated—as if they didn't exist past as far as you could reach. But their limbs were reaching steadfastly skyward and resembled elongated hands. The birds in those limbs were every brilliant colour you could imagine, and their song was like musical laughter. The sky was full of myriad pillows drifting overhead, and the sun was not so much a sphere as a wondrous, beautifully undulating, multi-coloured fire in the heavens.

Addie spent several minutes staring at one of her hands, then the other, flexing her fingers and marveling at their function. But where was she? It certainly wasn't Liverpool. Was it heaven? Was she dead? Where was Patrick? Would she ever see Papa—or Fedor again?

As Addie pulled herself upright, a dozen little flickering

lights began swarming about her merrily. They were not insects and were too small to have faces, but Addie could hear them whisper to each other.

"Is it her?" asked one tiny voice.

"Yes, yes it is!" another replied excitedly.

These frenetic creatures amazed and delighted Addie. "Who are you?" she asked them, then realized how impolite she sounded. Regardless, it was to no avail.

"Quickly! We must tell the others." The swarm chattered among themselves, circled about Addie several times, and hurriedly disappeared over the hill.

Addie called after them, "Wait! What others? Where are you going?" But they were gone. Puzzled, Addie began to explore her environment further. She wandered over to the nearby slow-moving stream, crouched down, and gazed in wonder at her reflection as it swirled and distorted around the stones.

"Could that be me?" She thought. "Do I wiggle and swirl like that?"

To her amazement, one of the stones in the stream sat up to reveal that it was not a stone at all, but rather a large, friendly-looking turtle. Seeing her, he stood up on his hind legs in the shallow water, becoming about two feet tall:

"Welcome, Miss Addie."

"Hello," Addie answered reflexively. Then, before she even realized it, she found herself asking, "Are you a turtle or a terrapin?" She blanched again at how forward and impertinent she was being. "Oh, sorry. That was rude." But beyond that particular turtle-terrapin mystery, she suddenly realized how odd it was that the turtle was not only speaking, but addressing *her*... and he knew her name!

"Do I know you?" she pressed him. "What happened to Patrick?"

"I uh…don't know, Miss Addie," admitted the puzzled turtle.

"But he was right behind me," insisted Addie.

The turtle looked roundabout. "Well, I don't see him. But of course, you were running away from him anyway…"

"He can run so much faster than--wait, how did you know that?" asked Addie.

The turtle opened his mouth to answer, but upon glancing up at her, he suddenly became wide-eyed, "What is *that* on your finger?!"

Addie looked at her hand and found that she was still wearing the signet ring Fedor had given her. "This? Why Prince Fedor gave this to me."

"Prince Fedor? *Our* Prince Fedor? Where did you last—?"

Addie interrupted; suddenly, she needed to know: "Please tell me: What *is* this place?"

The turtle cleared his throat, "You are in the kingdom of Ziymia, Your Highness," he calmly told her.

"Highness?" she exclaimed. Maybe Fedor had indeed made her a princess! Then she realized what else the turtle had just said and beamed instantly. "You mean I made it? I made it to Ziymia? Somehow, I knew it. It's as beautiful as Fedor described it!" She paced around with her arms out and a broad smile, trying to take it all in. But then she recalled her primary goal: "May I see him? Can you take me to Fedor?"

The turtle suddenly seemed very uneasy. "There is a standing decree from the palace, Your Highness. When the 'One to come' arrives, she is to proceed directly to the royal palace."

"The royal palace? Of course! That would be where Fedor lives," she noted to herself. "Wait. Did you just say 'One to come'?" asked Addie, puzzled.

"You're the One in the Oracle, are you not?

"Oracle?" Addie was getting more confused.

The turtle raised his finger, "I'm sure I have a copy. One moment." With that, his head and arms disappeared into his shell. Addie could hear the sound of shuffling papers and opening and closing desk drawers coming from within. Presently, the turtle returned with a small scroll tied in a ribbon. He removed the ribbon, unrolled the parchment, and began to read:

"One shall come,
Both royal and fair,
To light the darkness,
Cast out despair,
Bring home the crown,
Restore the throne,
Brave fire and ice,
And then be gone."

Addie cast a skeptical eye toward the turtle. "So you think that little poem is talking about me?"

"Well, Your Highness, you're certainly 'royal and fair.' What else should I be thinking?"

"'Casting out despair, braving fire and ice'? How silly! That couldn't possibly be me," insisted Addie. The concept was absurd, and yet it clawed at her from the back of her mind—what if she *wasn't* master of her own destiny?

"I think one day you may surprise yourself," the turtle assured.

"Well, if I'm the princess," Addie resolved, "And the decree says I must go to the palace, I suppose that is where I shall need to go. Mr. Turtle, will you take me there? Perhaps Fedor can explain all this Oracle business." The turtle marched out of the water onto dry land and bowed politely.

"I am your loyal subject, Your Highness."

Addie stepped back and looked at him with hands on her hips and a grin. "I never had a turtle for a subject before."

He became unsure of himself and cast his eyes down, "Do… do you want to *change* the subject?"

"Oh no…Who'd want to change a fine, handsome turtle like yourself?"

The turtle's expression now shone with pride. If turtles blushed, he certainly would have, but there's no telling what colour it might have been in the land of Ziymia.

"Thank you, Your Highness." Then he whispered, "But actually…I'm a terrapin."

"Why, of *course* you are!" Addie blurted out and smiled. "You're walking on land. That makes you a terrapin. I knew that!"

The terrapin then grew more serious, "Now that we've settled that question, Your Highness, it's a rather long journey to the palace, as I understand."

"Well, then, we should be getting started. But if we're going to be traveling together, I'd like to at least know who you are. What's your name, Mr. Turtle…er…Terrapin?" Addie asked.

"I don't have one yet. What would you like it to be?"

"Well…I always wanted a brother to play with," she mused. "How about if I just call you…'Brother'?"

"'Brother' it is, Your Highness!" he smiled proudly.

"And you can call me Addie."

"Certainly, your Addie-ness."

"No," she giggled, "Just 'Addie'."

She stepped up to the crest of the stream bank and looked about. "Well, Brother, what's the best way to the palace?"

Brother started to squirm and rubbed his brow, "I'm afraid I…um…don't really…"

Suddenly, a myriad of the little glowing lights reappeared, swirling around Addie and Brother, making sounds that resembled melodic giggling.

"The Idgits!" Brother exclaimed. "Maybe they can help!"

The Idgits flew over and attached themselves to the broad

face of a large nearby rock. As they settled, their light faded away, and they became mere bumps on the surface.

Addie recognized the pattern of the bumps.

"Braille! A message in Braille…" she called out excitedly.

Brother looked at her hopefully, "What does it say?"

Addie focused intently on the array of bumps. "I…I can't read it with my eyes."

"Use your fingers, then," said Brother. He pulled a pencil and pad of paper out of his shell and stood at the ready, "Call out the letters, and I'll write them down." Addie closed her eyes and ran her fingers over the bumps to read them.

"D…O…N…O…," she called out.

"Yes, Your Highness, continue," urged Brother

"T…T…O…U…C…H," Addie finished.

Brother looked up from his notepad, "'Do not touch?'"

Addie opened her eyes and broke out laughing at the absurdity of a Braille sign with such a message. The Idgits leapt off the rock again and swirled around her, giggling, delighted to have entertained the new princess.

But Brother became indignant at the way their princess was being treated. He scolded the Idgits, "Very funny. I thought you were going to help. Idgits! Indeed!" he fumed.

Addie managed to curb her laughter and put on a stern face. "Yes, please, can you tell us which way to the royal palace?"

Immediately, the Idgits snapped back to the rock, this time forming an arrow pointing to Addie's right. She nodded her approval to them with a smile. "Oh! That's much better, thank you."

With that, Addie and Brother embarked on a journey through the fantastical landscape, following the sun. Addie merrily took in the wonders of this land, taking care to absorb everything around her, even walking backward to look behind her. She couldn't stop basking in the joy, not only of seeing, but in the freedom of walking and running without using her cane.

They had not gone very far when suddenly, Addie cried out, terror-stricken: "Aauuugh! Brotherrrr! I…I've got a dark thing following me! It's sticking to my feet. Brother, *help* me!" She tried to run away but could not outpace it.

"Addie, stop!" Brother pleaded loudly and smiled. "Look at me." Addie halted and did as he asked. "See? I've got one too!" he pointed at his feet. She exhaled a bit.

Sure enough, he *did* have one. Now, she was puzzled.

"Addie, it's called a shadow. Everybody's got one. But they only come out when the sun is shining. There have always been shadows."

"You mean it's all right? Wh…why didn't they tell me about shadows when I was blind?"

Brother shrugged. "I guess you didn't need to know." He resumed his journeying toward the sun.

Addie followed him but, after a few paces, paused and smiled to herself. She turned around and pronounced: "It's so nice to make your acquaintance, Miss Shadow! I just *know* we're going to be the best of friends." She turned back to face the sun, but then, over her shoulder with a smirk, "We're going on to the palace now. You may come if you wish."

As expected, her shadow dutifully followed Addie and Brother on their journey.

Fedor slowly awakened in the room that Charlie had taken for them at the Hotel Terrapin in the heart of the city of Manchester. It was late in the morning, and the traffic sounds from outside—horse hooves and clattering wood-and-metal wheels on cobblestones—finally nudged him to wakefulness.

Soon after that, Fedor heard the sound of footsteps coming up the wooden stairs, followed by Charlie entering the room carrying some small packages and finding Fedor sitting on the edge of his bed. "Oh, g'mornin,' Lad. I brought breakfast. You want the porridge or the fish?" Charlie unpacked several containers from the larger package.

"Porridge, please," yawned Fedor. "Did you send the telegram yet, Charlie?"

"Not yet, Lad. As soon as you're all set up here, I'll go do that. I saw the telegraph office just down the way." Charlie began placing the food containers on a small table, along with a serving of bread, jam, and a tin of tea. "You're still worried about the girl?"

Fedor nodded.

"Well, I'll check up on it—but you're gonna owe me, Lad," Charlie winked. "I'll be off then." He picked up the package of paper-wrapped fried fish but then put it back down. "Oh, I almost forgot," he said, reaching for his wallet and placing a bill and several coins on the table. "Here's your allowance." He then retrieved one of the coins from the table, displayed it, and pocketed it once again in his vest. "…less the cost of the telegram. After the telegraph office, I'll be over at the pub. Try to keep yourself out of trouble, Lad."

"I'll be all right, Charlie."

Charlie put on his bowler, grabbed his fish breakfast, and scurried out the door.

As Fedor sat down and began to spoon his porridge, his mind swam with thoughts of Addie. The vivid memories of her smile alternated with clouds of worry from his nightmare last night. But was it a nightmare? It certainly felt like more than that.

After finishing breakfast, he dressed himself and prepared to go out to explore the city, hoping the new sights and sounds would distract his thoughts. He brushed his ample hair into submission and donned his hooded cloak. He made sure that he had his allowance in his pocket and headed down the stairs into the bustling thoroughfares of downtown Manchester.

At first Fedor simply ambled down the sidewalk. His hood shielded him well enough from undue attention, and he was able to take in the sounds and smells of this vibrant metropolis. But the vibrant energy of life in the noisy street soon became wearying even though it had the desired effect of clearing his brain.

Before long, his journey took Fedor past a small local church. The signboard outside proclaimed, "Sunday Sermon: 'The Kingdom of Heaven.'" It wasn't Sunday, so he probably wouldn't hear that sermon. But it made him think of the fanciful kingdom he himself had constructed in Addie's imagination, which had, in turn, resulted in an excited and cheerful girl with a glorious smile. He decided that her smile was his very own Kingdom of Heaven. Though his performances entertained people and even made them smile, rarely had he been able actually to bring personal joy to another person. And he liked how it made him feel.

Fedor entered the chapel, seeking temporary refuge from the street's clamor, his cloak being less conspicuous there than almost anywhere, and sat for a short time in a rear pew. After absorbing the peaceful quiet and the faint smell of incense—

which was far better than the odors in the street—Fedor found himself gazing up at all the figures of the saints perched on the walls about him. They made him wonder if he would be judged for deceiving Addie with the stories about his identity. If he was, he was determined to gladly accept such a judgment, as the satisfaction of providing Addie with even fleeting happiness was more than worth it to him.

Chapter Ten

Before long, Addie and Brother came to a garden where all the plants and trees bore fruit that consisted of household objects. There were feather-duster trees, shoe-horn bushes, candlestick plants, and hearth-bellows flora. Addie took notice.

"I always wondered where things like these came from," Addie said to herself and admired several shrubs that bore dozens of little opened umbrellas. "Brother, what do you call these?"

Brother glanced over and answered, "That's a stand of umbrella trees…and over there…" he smiled, "…is a tree of umbrella stands…" He pointed across the way, and sure enough, that was just what Addie saw.

"…and look at this," noted Addie as she stepped over to pluck the fruit of another tree. It resembled a small jewelry box. "What do you suppose is in these boxes?"

She cracked open the lid and peals of silly laughter poured out of the box. Addie couldn't help but chuckle at the sound of it.

"It's just a case of the giggles," Brother told her matter-of-factly—which only made her laugh more. "Come on now. We must get you to the palace," he urged. "They'll be expecting us." He turned and headed beyond the garden to continue their journey. Addie smiled in amusement, shook her head, and followed Brother.

As they walked along, Addie began wondering. "Brother?"

"Yes, Your Highness?" He said patiently, facing forward as he walked.

"How did I get here, in Ziymia?"

Brother stopped, looked at her, and stroked his chin. "All I know is I was cooling myself in that stream, and before I knew it, there you were," he shrugged. "So I'm afraid I don't really know how you got here, Your Highness. Perhaps they can tell us at the Palace."

Addie hadn't thought of that. She nodded, "I'm sure you're right. Let's be on our way, then." She took his hand, and they continued walking.

By and by, they passed through a big clearing followed by another grouping of differently-coloured bushes and trees that were all sprouting tableware. One shrub bore forks and knives, another bowls, another cups, and plates.

Addie's face brightened, "I think I've heard of this place!" she explained excitedly.

Brother looked up at her as she plucked a fork off a bush.

"This must be the Garden of Eatin'!" she laughed, very proud of herself.

Brother was not amused, rolling his eyes and continuing the march towards the sun.

"Oh, Brother, don't be so serious," Addie followed, trying to coax him.

"There is a time and place for everything, Your Highness," He said. "For now, we must be about your royal business."

"Oh, you're as bad as Rachel," Addie muttered as they walked.

"I beg your pardon, Your Highness?" Brother queried, not quite understanding.

"Never mind," Addie conceded, sighing. "You're correct, of course. Royal business." She was starting to realize that Brother might not be the playmate she had hoped for.

The landscape soon began to exhibit even more vivid hues, and Addie and Brother found themselves in an area where much of the ground had small and medium-sized toys lying about; blocks, balls, tops, dolls, and toy musical instruments abounded, all shiny, new, and full of colour. Curious, Addie paused to pick up a small rubber ball.

"Now, Brother, how can you be so grim when there are all these wonderful bits of fun in this place?"

But to Addie's surprise, a voice came from the very ball in her hand, "It's all for you, Your Highness."

"Oh!" she gasped.

Startled, she let go of the ball. It dropped and then bounced up to a point in space not far away, hovering there.

No sooner had the ball found its place in the air than many more of the nearby small objects jumped up to join with it until, finally, the mass of coloured blocks, spinning tops, jacks, and marbles came to form a shape that resembled a man.

Addie watched in amazement. Brother cowered behind her, his head half submerged in his shell.

Once complete, the man of toys bowed to Addie, "Welcome, Your Highness."

Addie could hardly believe what she was seeing. "Who are you?"

"You can call me Toybox," he informed her, juggling three different-coloured balls as he spoke. "Won't you stay and play awhile, Your Highness?"

Addie looked at Brother, who, as expected, was wearing his face of skepticism. His glance made her admit to herself that she was probably getting too old for such childish playthings. She was becoming a woman, after all, and would soon have both womanly and royal responsibilities. She turned back to Toybox. "I'm afraid we can't, Toybox. We're on our way to the palace."

"Er...royal business, you understand," chimed in Brother, stepping out from behind Addie. "So don't you try to hold us up now, Toybox," he scolded.

Addie tried to soften it to be more polite, "Yes, I'd love to stay, but I..." Just then, something new caught Addie's eye. "What is *that*?"

A strange procession had seized Addie's attention: A line of a half dozen robed and hooded figures, each about Addie's size, floated along, hovering four feet off the ground. The lead figure held a beautiful and brilliant beacon in outstretched hands before him. Their faces were all hidden in their hooded robes, and they passed by fairly quickly, taking no apparent notice of Addie and company.

"Those are the Keepers...they report to the King," Brother explained. "They continually roam over the land. They're said to have mysterious powers. And no one that I know has ever seen their faces."

"What's that he's carrying, the one in front?" asked Addie.

"That's the Royal Flame; it's—"

Addie was excited, "Then they must be going to the Palace! Come on, we can follow them!" Addie started to run after the Keepers, with Brother following as best he could. Addie paused and looked back to call out to a motionless Toybox, "Are you coming, Toybox?"

"Am I!?" exuded Toybox, elated that he, too, had been invited on the adventure. He elongated his legs so he could take longer strides to catch up with Addie and Brother.

Addie so admired the beauty and merriment of this land that she found herself wanting to live here forever. *"Forever?"* she asked herself, almost as soon as the thought crossed her mind. But she was reminded that it felt like no one really wanted her around at home. But still, what if she ever *did* want to go home? *"I suppose the answer to that can probably be found at the palace also,"* she told herself. Addie bent down, picked up Brother, and lifted him to her shoulders. "Come on, Brother, we have to get to the palace," she urged as they picked up the pace.

The trio hurriedly progressed through the land, leaving the toys behind. But now the environment was beginning to be dotted with oversized items that all seemed to be for games: giant jackstraws, stacks of two-foot diameter red and black checkers, jump ropes the size of pythons, old maid playing cards, and ring toss rings. The more crowded the path became with these beckoning ornaments of play, the slower the group's progress. The Keepers, though, seemed to be slipping out of reach toward the horizon.

An out-of-breath, Addie urged, "We're losing them. We need to hurry." She began to move faster even though she was tiring quickly.

Suddenly, a booming voice echoed across the valley, "Simon

says STOP!" and a wall of six-foot dominoes abruptly sprouted in front of them, cutting off any further travel.

This turn of events shocked Addie and frightened her a little. For the first time in this land she felt uneasy, even a slight tinge of homesickness. She let Brother down off her shoulders. "What do we do *now*?" she lamented, nearly in tears. Brother paced up and down, looking for a passage through the wall—or some other solution. Toybox attempted to comfort Addie as she sat down on an oversized pair of dice to rest and consider options.

Almost unnoticed by the group, the domino directly in front of them swung open like a gate, and from it emerged a gregarious and wildly-dressed thin man with a wide-brimmed blue hat, purple frazzled hair, and orange plaid trousers. His overall appearance was distinctly clownish, and his eyes seemed permanently open wide.

"I don't remember anybody saying, 'Simon says look tired and sad,'" said the man. "You obviously need to have some fun. Shall we play 'Simon Says?'"

"Why?" scowled Brother, not in the mood for this.

"Because I'm *Simon,* and I *say*, that's why," the clownish man pouted.

"Mister Simon, we need to get to the royal palace," Addie pleaded. "It's grownup stuff—so please excuse us." She ran her fingers over the smooth domino wall, still seeking an opening.

"Aww, just one little game," pleaded Simon. "It won't take a minute. It'll be lots of fun; you'll be refreshed and on your way! What do you say?" Simon's attitude had gone from petulant toddler to exuberant harlequin in mere moments.

Addie and Brother glanced at each other, seeking clues as to how to handle this fellow, when Toybox spoke up, "That sounds terrific!"

"Toybox!" Brother and Addie growled in unison, rolling their eyes.

"That's better," Simon gushed, "I knew you'd come around."

Addie glowered at exuberant Toybox, his smile fading once he noticed the disapproval of his companions.

"Now come on, everybody, get in a line. Come on, come on, come on," bounced Simon. Reluctantly, Addie, Brother, and Toybox lined up parallel to the wall of dominoes. Simon took his place in front of them. "That's good! Everybody ready? Now, Simon says 'put your hands on your head.'"

The group dutifully placed their hands on their heads. Brother sighed.

"Simon says, 'Clap your hands.'"

The group clapped.

"Touch your knees!" Simon said. But nobody did so. He smiled a fiendish grin. Oooohh, you think you're all clever, don't you? Well, let's continue."

Addie and Brother stood at the ready. Toybox bounced up and down like an anxious puppy. Simon paused, lowering his head as he eyed the group, preparing to launch his next command.

"Simon says…*climb a mountain and eat spaghetti!*"

A look of horror came over Toybox, who desperately wanted to play the game. His eyes darted left and right in befuddlement while Addie and Brother merely glared at Simon.

"C'mon, you're not playing!" Simon whined, "We're losing all the fun. Come on!" He continued: "Simon says…*swing from a chandelier and dig to China!*"

Again, all he got was stares.

After a quick glance at Brother, Addie stepped forward out of the ranks and approached Simon. "Simon," she spoke softly. "I have a secret to share with you."

"Oh! Secrets!" clapped the clown with his gloved hands.

"Simon, listen to me," continued Addie, drawing near to his ear and whispering, "You make more friends if you *help* other people than if you force them to do what *you* want." Having delivered the message, she stepped back.

Simon's face went blank as he used whatever small brain power he had to try to process what Addie had told him. At last, he spoke boldly: "Simon says…'Pass!'"

And at once, the domino wall fell away in a wave from left to right. Addie and Brother hugged while Toybox hopped up and down with joy and clapped.

"At last! That's better," grumbled Brother.

"Thank you, Simon!" Addie called out as the travelers immediately continued on their journey, leaving Simon behind.

"Wait!" Simon shouted at the receding trio. Addie and her friends paused and turned back to face Simon. "You didn't say 'Mother, may I?'" He then broke into peals of hysterical laughter, bouncing and doing cartwheels all over the area. Addie and her friends shook their heads and returned to their travels, determinedly moving toward the horizon, while Simon's manic cackling gradually faded in the distance behind them.

Addie noted to herself that if she'd been told not long ago that she would be tiring of fun and games, she would never have believed it.

Quiet quickly descended over the Land of Games after the three departed, and tranquility ruled there for a few precious moments.

Unseen by Addie or any of her companions, however, and not long after they departed Simon, a violent, dark wind quickly rose out of nowhere and soon swept through that very area in the Land of Games, ripping its very substance into minute black particles, devolving into a roiling, thick liquid as it settled, finally dissipating into black, empty, nothingness. That part of the kingdom was no more.

Chapter Eleven

Addie's injured body lay unconscious in the converted master bedroom of the Alexander residence. The room had been hastily reconfigured as a convalescent room due to its larger size, ground-floor accessibility, better light, and larger bed than Addie's own bedroom on the upper floor offered.

A substantial bandage was on one side of Addie's head, with several other minor scratches and abrasions on her face. She was alone except for Ezra, his mind overflowing with memories, guilt, and fears as he sat motionless at her bedside. Weighing even more heavily on him was sheer physical exhaustion; for the theatre didn't run itself. It was a business that sorely needed his guiding and forceful hand to keep it from spiraling into chaos. Yet Addie was his treasure and now needed his full-time attention. Raising any child and running a business would be a challenge. But the needs of a blind child made the balance even more difficult. And now there was no way he would leave her side.

The theatre would simply have to continue operating, and he would have to hope that his staff was up to the task. But of further concern was that times like this would be even more bleak in the coming days after Rachel departed their lives.

There was a gentle knock on the open door. Ezra looked up to see that it was Rachel.

"Hello, Ezra. I came as soon as I heard."

Ezra found himself exhaling a sigh of relief. "Rachel, come in please." He rose to offer his seat—the chair by Addie's side.

"Thank you, Ezra. How is she?" Rachel sat and took Addie's hand.

"No change, really," Ezra replied. "It's maddening. She just doesn't respond!" He stepped away to the window. "The doctor says it could be weeks, months, even years…" Ezra choked on the words and could not finish his sentence. He faced the window so that Rachel would not see his tears. After a moment of composing himself, he added, "I just feel as if this would never have happened if I hadn't been so…"

"Oh, nonsense," interrupted Rachel. "There's no point in assigning blame or worrying about what might have been." Rachel's very presence brought an aura of peace to the room. She lightly caressed Addie's forehead as Ezra looked on. "Poor troubled angel. She's just a sleeping beauty, Ezra." She looked up to assure him, "She'll wake soon."

"If she does, do you think she'll ever forgive me?" asked Ezra.

Rachel touched his hand. "Only if you're willing to forgive yourself, Ezra."

Ezra tried to understand. His voice started to raise, "How can you be so…strong, so stable at a time like this?"

"I'm not strong, Ezra," Rachel explained. "But I have faith. Just yesterday morning, Pastor Fisher told us that faith is like a flower blooming in the desert."

Ezra couldn't look her in the eye.

Rachel turned back to Addie and began softly to hum a familiar song: "Beautiful Dreamer." The emotion of hearing one of Addie's favourite melodies was almost more than Ezra could take. He had to retreat into the hallway to weep.

Addie, Toybox, and Brother continued their journey in pursuit of the Keepers, oblivious to either the destruction that had occurred behind them or the somber scene where Addie's broken body lay in her home. Their route had taken them through a lush valley, full of grasses and flowers.

As they walked, Addie suddenly became aware of a two-foot

translucent sphere embedded in the hillside. "What's this?" she puzzled. It had a golden shimmering light coming from inside.

"Here's another one!" exclaimed Brother, a few feet away, standing over a one-foot sphere of a different color.

"…and another!" piped up Toybox a little further down the valley.

When they raised their eyes to look, the landscape ahead of them became more and more populated with the lovely spheres.

Just then, however, the hovering procession of Keepers re-appeared, heading towards the group, looping around, and then returning to the direction from which they had come. Addie began to run after them, calling out as she ran: "Wait, please! We want to come too!" But soon, the Keepers were far beyond what Addie could ever hope to catch up with. She finally had to stop and catch her breath as she watched the robed figures disappear over the hill.

Addie sat down to rest on a nearby sphere—In fact, the surrounding terrain now appeared to consist entirely of spheres of various sizes.

"Looks like we can have a ball here!" said Toybox excitedly, juggling an elaborate pattern of five balls, each changing colour as they cycled through his hands. "What shall we play now, Your Highness?"

"Oh, Toybox, I…"Addie began, but then her ears noticed something: the distant strains of many instruments playing "Beautiful Dreamer."

"Listen!… What's that?" she asked, standing up to hear more clearly.

Toybox stretched himself to be much taller in order to see over the hill. He called down to Addie, "It's the music of the spheres! Looks like they're having a festival just over this hill."

Addie looked up to find colourful "music" flowing like honey into the sky from a point just beyond the steep hill of spheres before them. Toybox shrank back down to normal height.

"If the music can play, so can we!" said Toybox. "What're we waiting for?" He leapt to the top of a good-sized spherical "boulder" and held out a hand for Addie to grab.

"But…it's such a long climb," she sighed. She glanced over at Brother, who, to his astonishment —and hers—began rising into the air like a balloon!

"Don't worry about the hill," explained Toybox, "Gravity's optional for holidays and festivals. Come on!" Addie took Toybox's hand, and they both floated skyward as well.

Exhilarated, Addie could scarcely believe what was happening. As they ascended, Addie and Toybox passed by Brother, who was attempting to swim downward to get his feet back on the ground.

"But Addie, the palace…" he pleaded.

Addie took Brother's hand and pulled him along back into the sky. "Don't you see, Brother? We can get there faster this way!"

Toybox transformed the shape of all his bits and pieces, rearranging them to form "wings," which he flapped to keep pace with his friends.

As they rose above the ridge, a magnificent valley came into view, with huge musical instruments jutting out of the terrain like great monoliths. A gigantic band organ was the centre of it all, from which flowed a steady stream of ever-changing colour, along with dozens of bright spheres, that floated like bubbles into the sky.

Addie, Brother, and Toybox exuberantly explored the valley from their aerial vantage point, swimming through the sky as the music ebbed and flowed, splashing through the colourful harmonies, and playfully immersing themselves in the melody emanating from the over-sized instruments. The rising spheres swirled and weaved around the soaring Addie and her companions as if dancing, joining with the trio in a musical revelry.

Soon, however, like the end of a carousel ride, the music wound to a close; the colourful river of harmony that had been flowing into the sky now dissipated, and the companions drifted back to the ground. Toybox transposed back into his human-like form as he descended.

"Aww…we were just starting to have some real fun," Toybox whined.

"No, we were just starting to make some *progress* toward the palace," Brother corrected.

"Oh, but it was wonderful!" Addie sighed. "Of course, if the music kept going, *we* could keep going too…" She glanced up at the huge band organ. Sure enough, it had a slot for a penny…but sadly, there were no pennies to be had in her pockets.

"Looking for one of these?" offered Toybox as he plucked a penny from its position among all the other miscellany that made up his torso.

Addie joyfully clapped her hands and smiled broadly. Brother couldn't help but observe just how extra pretty she was when she was smiling. He knew he'd do almost anything to keep that smile going.

"Well, go on, Toybox," Brother urged. "Drop it in the slot."

Given the enormous size of the band organ, Brother knew Toybox was the only one of the group capable of reaching high enough to feed the coin into the machine. He simply stood at its base and elongated himself until he was able to reach the slot, deftly dropping the coin into its place.

Immediately—and to Addie's delight—a new melody began to play: an ornate and flowery version of what Addie recognized as a classic hymn. She and her companions once more began rising skyward, elated at the resumption of their freedom from the confines of gravity. But Addie's brow took on a slight furrow, "I…think I *know* this song."

"Oh?" said Brother, kicking past her as if in water, "What is it, then?"

Addie sighed, "Somehow, I just can't seem to remember the words."

"Does it matter?" Toybox chimed in. "You're enjoying yourself, aren't you?"

"I'm sure it'll come to you," reassured Brother. "Try humming along. Maybe the music will lead you to the words."

Addie wondered if her memories of home were somehow slipping away. She looked up at the musical river of colour and its accompanying spheres flowing overhead. It was now flowing in a specific direction, heading over the horizon. "Maybe the music *can* lead us!" she exclaimed, "It's flowing the same way we're going, so let's follow it."

With that, the three began to soar higher and higher, passing through layers of pillow clouds until their altitude was well above the wide and colourful River of Harmony. As they drifted placidly along with it, they gained a new bird's eye view of the land of Ziymia while following the aerial river in its journey toward the horizon.

Before long, the land of music had drifted behind them, and they floated over several multi-hued landscapes. Soon, the ground far below them began to look very much like…no, *exactly like*, a down quilt! With its calico, plaid, and polka-dotted squares, it appeared as an enormous bedspread, and so to Addie seemed a tranquil place.

Pointing to the huge quilt landscape, she asked Brother, "What do you call that?"

"Shhh!" Brother cautioned, whispering, "The sooner we're past it, the better…It's called…uh…Bedlam."

Surprised, Addie whispered back, "Bedlam? That sounds… noisy. But it looks so calm."

"It's the land of *pillow fights!*" shouted Toybox, who had grabbed a "cloud" and whacked Brother with it, sending him tumbling end over end into another "cloud bank" of pillows and scattering them on impact. Addie giggled along with Toybox, who was now laughing so hard he didn't even notice that a pillow-wielding Brother was barreling back at him at high speed.

Brother impacted Toybox, shattering him into his respective pieces. He then discarded his pillow and turned to Addie. "That ought to teach him. Toybox simply *has* to learn that aggression only leads to more aggression…*YAAH!*"

Unseen by Brother, the pieces of Toybox had quickly re-assembled to form a multi-spoked "pillow fight contraption" with half a dozen pillows whirling around its rim, now headed straight for him. He began running—which in a weightless condition was rather awkward. A bemused Addie looked on as they chased each other around her.

"Addie! Your Highness…heeeelp!" yelled Brother.

But something in the distance caught Addie's notice. "Brother, Toybox, look!" She pointed.

The pair ceased their conflict as they all realized that the River of Harmony was now flowing downward—them along with it—and its end was coming into sight.

As they descended along with the undulating river, they

observed that it was condensing and coalescing to form delicious-looking—if oddly coloured—foodstuffs, which were so large that they seemed to consume the countryside as the descending river merged into it. Meringue pies loomed as hills; huge pastries dotted the horizon; tree-sized candy canes abounded, with countless cookies and bonbons of all sizes and colours scattered over the landscape.

"Oh, how wonderful!" exclaimed Addie. "And just in time, too; I'm dreadfully hungry."

"Me too!" agreed Toybox as he tossed some bits of hard candy into his "mouth."

"You can't be hungry, Toybox," noted Brother, "You don't even have a stomach."

Sure enough, the candies just bounced around off the bits and pieces that comprised Toybox's mid-section, finally dropping to the ground. Toybox watched the process attentively.

"Oh yeah…" he admitted sheepishly.

Addie pulled off a portion of a nearby cupcake and began to nibble, offering up a piece to Brother. "How about you, Brother? Would you like some?"

"No, thank you," said Brother. "I'm just a bit thirsty."

"There's a soda fountain over there…" offered Toybox. And so there was: a great purple bubbling one, with statues of cherubs and nymphs decorating the fountain's spouts around a big gurgling pond.

Brother stepped over to the fountain. He was feeling a bit uneasy about the group's slowed progress. "Just a moment of refreshment before we move on," he promised as he sipped from the pool of sparkling soda.

Addie sat down in the shade at the base of a large candy cane. The moment she did so, she found herself overcome with a yawn. "Couldn't we rest just a little while? It's so quiet here."

And indeed it was, with the grove of candy canes beside the slowly meandering multi-flavored river.

"But Addie, we need to keep…" Brother began. But it was already too late; her eyes were closed. Brother looked over at Toybox.

"She's the boss," Toybox shrugged. He, too, settled in under a cotton candy tree, leaving only a frustrated Brother standing. Helpless to do anything else, Brother paced a bit, then shook his head, threw up his arms, and resolved that he at least would continue to stand watch.

Ezra was sound asleep in the chair near Addie's bed. It was nighttime, the close of a third day of bedside vigil. At Ezra's elbow was a small table stacked with piles of contracts and other papers from his theatre's office.

Across the room, Rachel was doing needlework by the light of a kerosene lamp. These events had certainly dampened her enthusiasm about leaving Addie to engage in her new position. She mentally rehearsed the many scenarios that might transpire in the coming days and weeks. She was certainly concerned about Addie at this time of trial, yet she also wanted to do her best by the other children with whom she would soon be entrusted. But she couldn't decide which was more of her Christian duty and which was of her own personal desire. And in taking this new position, was she betraying her promise to Annabelle? Suddenly, everything was less clear than it had been before.

And then there was Ezra, Rachel mused as she gazed at him slumped over in this fleeting moment of peace. Even in this rumpled state of stolen rest, he somehow exuded an air of dignity. He was a steadfast man and probably a better father to Addie than he would admit to. And that endeared him to Rachel more than *she* would care to concede.

Patrick entered the home by its front door and made his way to Addie's room, removing his hat and whispering to Rachel, "It's me."

Rachel welcomed him, "Hello, Patrick. Come in."

"The show just got out, and I came right over," Patrick said. "How's she doing?"

"The doctor examined her earlier. He doesn't see any broken bones either in her head or otherwise, so we're thankful for that," Rachel told him. "He even changed her bandage for a smaller one."

"I…um, brought this for her." Patrick took Addie's well-worn stuffed turtle from beneath his coat and placed it next to her in the bed, kneeling solemnly at her side, crossing himself.

Addie's body remained motionless.

Chapter Twelve

In the Land of Sweets, Brother had finally given in and slept peacefully by Addie's side. The sun was a bit lower in the sky. But a brilliant light began to shine on Addie's face, so bright that it woke her. She squinted into the brilliance to discover the Keepers, Royal Beacon in hand, hovering over her silently.

"Hello?" she asked, groggily.

But as soon as the Keepers realized she was aware of their presence, they quickly retreated, gliding off into the distance where they paused and hovered, waiting.

"Brother! Toybox!" Addie called, "It's the Keepers. Look!"

Brother and Toybox roused themselves and stood by Addie, gazing at the Keepers.

"It looks like they want us to follow them. I think they're waiting for us," Brother opined.

"I think you're right," agreed Addie, "Let's see what they want!" She began to run with Brother and Toybox in tow.

. . .

So the three caught up to the Keepers, who led them through a countryside that gradually transitioned from the glorious Land of Sweets into something more bleak and foreboding. Foliage was becoming more scarce and was often crumpled and broken. Scattered debris hindered their path, and they sometimes had to climb over it.

Toybox looked around with trepidation at the deteriorating countryside, "Addie? Are we sure we want to leave the Land of Sweets?" Addie gave him an accusing stare. Toybox got the message. "Um, like I was saying," he whimpered, "This sure is…interesting scenery…"

Though she wouldn't admit it, Addie was starting to agree with Toybox's trepidation. In the distance, though, she could begin to detect some sort of village, or at least remnants of one. As they came nearer, they could hear distant shouting and an occasional crash. Addie winced at the noise. It felt as though this was a different land, rather than part of Ziymia. She wondered why the area seemed so troubled.

"This doesn't look like much fun anymore," pouted Toybox, timidly bringing up the rear.

"I wonder why the Keepers have led us here," Addie pondered. Were they being led into a trap? Were they supposed to fix something in this rather desolate place? If so, what could it possibly be, and how could she and her friends even begin to correct what was obviously a terribly troubled place?

As they approached the village more closely, they could make out multiple structures, most of which seemed to be damaged. Around the enclave, there was a dilapidated fence and a worn and weathered sign.

When they came nearer, the sounds of angry voices spilled out constantly through the fence. When the group came near the sign, Brother could just make out the faded letters reading "Verbogen."

"Verbogen…I know about this place! There's been strife brewing here for many years," Brother explained. "It's the village of the blind."

Addie was startled, "The blind?! Why, this was what Prince Fedor wanted my help with!"

Just then, a mass of smelly debris from the village landed at Addie's feet, frightening the group.

"Couldn't we j-just go around this place?" asked Toybox, symbolically walking in a circle while his head remained facing Addie.

Addie sternly put her hands on her hips. "Now, Toybox, it may be frightening, but I made a promise to Prince Fedor that I would try to help these people. It's the whole reason why I came here." She tried her best to be brave about it, but she wondered to herself if she could even do anything for them, and if she might be risking letting Fedor down.

Another salvo of rubbish landed at their feet, causing the group to scatter. "Brother," Addie asked. "Why are these people so angry?"

"Mostly because they can't make progress on anything, I imagine," Brother said as he surveyed the grounds. "Folks want a better life, but they can't get it if they have to spend all their time feuding with their neighbors."

"But what's the problem? Why are they feuding?" insisted Addie.

"The good news is that nobody in Ziymia, let alone Verbogen, is totally blind. We have only certain *kinds* of blindness here," explained Brother.

"Kinds of blindness?" Addie asked.

"Some people, for instance, can't see beyond the end of their own nose. Others can't see anything to their right, and others can't see to their left. Another group can only see the big picture, while their rivals can only see details. Some can only see what's behind them."

"When I was blind," said Addie, "I would have been happy to only be partially blind like these people. To be partially blind means you can partially *see*. So why do they think they have to fight each other?"

"There are about a dozen different group homes in this village." Brother explained. "Each house is home to only one kind of blind people. Those who can't see to their right live in one home. All the ones that can't see to their left are in another. The idea is that they had common challenges so that they should be able to come up with group solutions. But each group began to isolate itself from the rest of the village and began warring with its neighbors."

"I think I understand…a little," said Addie, shifting her weight nervously.

"I believe His Majesty is concerned that if these problems are not worked out, the village might destroy itself…or cause problems for other parts of Ziymia," Brother concluded as Addie put her finger to her lip, thinking.

Suddenly, one of the residents, an aging man in a worn leather vest, collided with a younger, disheveled man just inside the fence. "Why ye errant pox-marked harpy!" the old man shouted at the younger. "Why don't ye watch where yer goin'?"

"I were watching' better'n you, ye impertinent miscreant!" yelled the younger. They stood sticking their chins out at each other until the old man waved his hand in disgust, "Bah!" and went on his way.

Brother exhaled, "I'm glad that one didn't go any farther."

With the peace at least temporarily maintained, Addie began to inspect the village from outside the fence, which was so porous as not to obstruct one's view. As Addie walked the perimeter, observing, Brother and Toybox followed a few paces behind her. If there was a solution here, it wasn't yet obvious. Perhaps as she understood the layout better, it might spark something. But the state of this village began to make her wonder— just a little—if this land was, in fact, someplace she would want to remain forever after all. But if she could help these people, even a little, it would make it all worthwhile.

Each of the dozen houses in the village appeared spacious enough for about twenty residents. The buildings were arranged around a large rectangle that was the central courtyard—though it was little more than a large patch of dirt. About fifty of the dusty village inhabitants could be seen wandering the courtyard. No one seemed happy or even energetic. But, for now at least, no one was yelling or attacking a neighbor. From what Addie had seen, though, such an outburst could come at any moment for any reason. If anything could be done, now was the time to do it.

"Brother," Addie began. "I have an idea, but we have to do it quickly. And I'll need your help. Yours too, Toybox."

"Here to serve, Your Highness," Brother acknowledged, while Toybox nodded in eager assent.

"I need to speak to the whole village," she explained. "Can you help arrange that?"

"We'll do our best, Miss Addie. Come on, Toybox." Brother and Toybox marched in through an opening in the fence and proceeded toward the front of a house with peeling paint that faced inward toward the courtyard. Addie followed along. The residents amazingly took no notice of these new visitors to their village.

"This looks like a good spot," said Brother. "Toybox, I need to get up there." He pointed to the roof.

"Gotcha, Boss," winked Toybox as he lowered his hand to the ground. Brother stepped aboard, and Toybox lifted and stretched to deliver the Terrapin to the roofline of the building. This would serve as a presentation platform.

Brother then instructed Toybox further. "You see that barrel? Bring that over here for Addie to stand on." Toybox complied and also moved a wooden box to act as a step up to the barrel for Addie.

"All right, Toybox, get their attention," waved Brother. Toybox looked puzzled for a moment until Addie pointed to a spot on her own torso that corresponded with the location of a whistle in Toybox's chest. Suddenly, he understood, plucked the whistle from its place, and blew it loudly. The piercing tone had the intended effect, and all the inhabitants now turned their faces toward the sound of the whistle. But those faces were blank, mostly from the ongoing weight of misery.

Brother loudly cleared his throat. "Citizens of Verbogen, please gather around. I want you all to meet our own Princess Addie." Addie stepped up to the top of the barrel, curtsied politely, and smiled. "She has something she wants to discuss with all of you," Brother proclaimed.

The residents became deathly quiet. Addie couldn't quite figure if that was good or bad. But she took the opportunity to try to keep their attention. "Greetings to you people of the realm. I come here at the invitation of Prince Fedor, our beloved Sovereign. He is well aware of the struggles that you all have with blindness, and he asked me if I could help you. The reason he asked me is that until recently, I, too, was blind, totally blind, and "Prince Fedor believed that my experience could assist you in your situation."

The old man in the leather vest sneered, "Aye and what's a wee lass like you gonter do to help *us*?" Other murmuring rippled through the group as well.

Addie swallowed nervously. "Please just listen for a moment, and maybe we can discover some new things together. Maybe you can even learn something about yourself and your neighbors." They quieted down a bit and fleetingly gave her their attention.

As she looked out over the crowd, Addie began to notice that the clothes they were wearing seemed to indicate the individual kinds of blindness they suffered from. Those who were blind on the right wore clothing that was black only on the right. Those who could only see behind wore black on the front. Those who couldn't see beyond the end of their nose had only a black circle on the tip of their noses. When this realization came to her, Addie then knew what she needed to do.

Addie raised her arms. "Now, I would like each of you to help me with a little contest and experiment," she said to the crowd. "Find a partner from your own group, someone with the same type of blindness as you. Go ahead…you know who they are." Addie watched as the citizens awkwardly paired up with partners.

"All right now, everyone line up along this edge of the court-yard," she indicated the long side of the rectangle. "And Toybox, could you draw us a finish line near the opposite edge of the field?" Toybox grabbed a stick and drew a line the length of the yard in the dirt.

"Now, everyone link arms with your partner," she continued, holding out her elbow to demonstrate. "And when Toybox blows his whistle again, race to the finish line as fast as you can. The first team over the line will be crowned champions."

"What're we going to crown them with?" whispered Brother to Addie.

"Don't worry. Just watch," she replied. Then to the group: "Everybody ready?"

Toybox readied his whistle. Addie counted: "One, two, three…"

Tweeeeeeet!

And the contest was on…but immediately it descended into chaos. Most of the two-person teams found themselves twirling in circles, with no one making any progress across the field at all. The noise level and shouting rose exponentially with the frustration of going nowhere. Addie finally decided to call it off before anyone came to blows. "Toybox?" she indicated. He nodded.

Tweeeeet!

Still, the chaos and tumult continued, completely ignoring Toybox's whistle. The conflict was beginning to get dangerous.

The old man in the leather vest took one of the younger men by the throat, "'Twere all your fault ye ignorant…"

Suddenly, a very bright flash of light and a deep pulsing sound from above caught everyone's attention. Addie looked up to see the Keepers, hovering twenty feet above the field formed in a circle around a central Keeper holding the Beacon, which was undoubtedly the source of the flash. With order restored, the Keepers backed away.

"Everyone go back to the starting line," Addie announced. Grumbling, they all gradually complied. "Now I want to try it a different way," she continued. I need two volunteers, one from the left-side group and one from the right-side group."

Knowing the animosity between the groups, she wasn't entirely certain there would be any volunteers. But having them agree to do this willingly was important. "Come on, just two volunteers. Nobody's going to bite you. I'll wait…" After a few more tense seconds, a hand at last went up from a left-sider. Not wanting to be outdone, a right-sider almost immediately followed suit.

"Wonderful! Come on over here, volunteers." She steered them to the centre of the starting line, clearing a few folks on either side so they'd have room. "Now left-sider on the left and right-sider on the right and…link your arms."

"What, with this blighter?" griped the left-sider. The crowd laughed nervously.

"Yes, with this gentleman," instructed Addie, smiling.

"All right…seeing as you're the princess," the left-sider conceded. The crowd chuckled more heartily.

"We're going to attempt to do the same race and see if we can do it faster than the last round."

"That shouldn't be hard," muttered Toybox.

"Ready now?" Addie announced. "One, two, three…"

Tweeeeeet!

The left and right side pair immediately launched straight ahead and was across the finish line in less than ten strides.

A huge cheer went up from all voices in the village. Brother and Toybox hugged each other, and Addie beamed, taking it all in. The other villagers hoisted the two participants on their shoulders and began parading them around the field.

After enjoying the revelry for a minute, Addie signaled to Toybox, who sounded his whistle once more, and the clamor subsided enough so that Addie could speak.

"I want you all to understand what just happened," announced Addie. "These were not extra special people. They didn't suddenly gain full eyesight. But I wanted you to understand that if someone can see things *you* can't see and you can see things they don't, it's better to work together, and you can win the race."

"How do we do that, Your Highness?" asked one right-sided woman standing nearby.

Addie smiled to herself, relieved that this was the question that was asked. "Well, as I understand it, in each of your houses you only live with others who have the same kind of blindness; is that so?" Everyone nodded. "So everyone in your house is missing the same things and makes the same mistakes." The crowd murmured agreement.

"So the answer is obvious!" Addie smiled, "It's moving day!

No house should have people with just one kind of blindness living there, but people with *every* kind. That way, you can all fill in the missing bits for each other. Everyone will be stronger, and you can rebuild your village to be more beautiful than ever. It's time to make some new friends."

The crowd was at first hushed. Then some murmuring began and Addie could see some heads bobbing in agreement. A few more left and right siders started pairing up to try out the concept. The murmuring continued growing stronger and now had a distinctly joyful feel to it. Addie and Brother looked at each other and smiled.

Once again Addie raised her arms and the crowd came to attention. "Now I know you're all smart and talented people. If you can all work together to do these simple changes I'm sure your lives will be much easier."

The crowd applauded. "Cheers for the princess!" they chanted, "Huzzah! Huzzah! Huzzah!" arose the exultation, over and over.

Toybox helped Brother down from the roof, and they joined Addie in celebration of the hope that Verbogen now had for its future.

But, as the throng surged, Addie looked up to discover the Keepers circling again. They began to slowly move away from the village as if to say, "Are you coming?"

"Looks like it's time to go if we're to keep up with the Keepers," Addie told Brother. Then she announced to the crowd, "I'm so glad we were able to be here to help you with your challenges. Some of you, I'm sure, still have doubts about cooperating with each other. But be patient and watch your neighbors. I'm certain you'll learn a few things. My partners and I now have royal business at the palace, and we must leave you for a while." A collective moan of disappointment went up from the crowd. Addie raised her arms to quiet them. "Be aware that we are all very proud of what you have accomplished here today. And we look forward to discovering all the marvelous things the people of this village will accomplish before the next time we come to visit you. Be patient with each other, and we'll join you again soon." She stepped down from the barrel and joined up with Brother and Toybox.

"Wonderful speech, Your Highness," praised Brother.

Toybox nodded. "Yeah! Coulda used a few more jokes, though."

The three began moving toward the perimeter. The disappointed crowd gave a collective sigh as they did so, but they soon transformed it into a round of applause. As Addie and her friends moved beyond the village fence, she turned, raised a finger, and spoke once more to the crowd with a wink. "And I want to see this fence all repaired and beautiful the next time we come to visit you."

The crowd laughed, applauded once more, and shed a little tear as Addie and company headed toward the horizon where the Keepers were waiting for them. A kindly lady in a blue scarf came running after them, offering a small sack containing some bread and a container of lemonade. "For your journey," she smiled and then waved as they left the village.

After they had walked a little way, Brother spoke, "Your Highness?"

"Yes?" Addie noticed Brother was smiling.

Brother continued, "It looks like you've brought:

'Light to the darkness
And cast out despair.'"

Addie scowled. "Brother, you don't still believe all that Oracle nonsense, do you?" She shook her head and kept walking ahead.

"I don't know, Your Highness—Do *you*?" asked Brother, still smiling.

Toybox gave Brother a playful nudge and a grinning thumbs up. The two followed after Addie.

As she walked along, a smile began to bloom on Addie's face. She felt proud as she reflected on what they had just achieved, basking in the knowledge that they had something good to report when they reached the palace.

But at the same time, she was haunted by the thought that Brother might be right, and perhaps the Oracle was actually true. And what would *that* mean? Was she merely a player going through steps that had been laid out for her long ago? Could she make *any* of her own choices? Did she even have a mind of her own? And who or what laid out those steps for her? And why?

She instinctively felt that such a Master Planner must undoubtedly be God. Who else could it be? But trying to understand His intentions along with her own responsibilities made her head swim.

As she pondered these things, though, she glanced up to find she had drifted behind her companions. She finally decided to set these matters aside for now and ran to catch up with her friends.

All three followed the Keepers as best they could and found themselves moving through a transitioning landscape. Behind them was the dried and crumpled land surrounding Verbogen; before them lay a nearly vacant expanse of smooth, perfectly flat land. Some craggy hills were in the distance, but all of the land was muted in tone and almost completely lacking in colour.

It all seemed so desolate that Addie began to wonder exactly what the "royal business" could be that was summoning her to the palace—if, in fact, they were ever to arrive there. But they *had* to make it there. And she was certain Fedor would answer her questions.

Despite their best efforts, however, Addie and her companions couldn't maintain the pace of the Keepers, who receded farther and farther into the distance. Addie was very tired and could observe that the long journey was taking its toll on Brother and Toybox as well.

"Time to rest," she finally admitted and sat down on the grey, flat surface of the ground.

"I wonder how much further it is," wondered Toybox.

Addie offered, "The Keepers have brought us this far. I'm sure they'll get us all the way."

"The sun is rather warm here," noticed Brother. "Mind if I take a break in the shade?"

"Shade?" Addie asked, squinting in the light.

"Just watch," said Brother , promptly withdrawing his head, tail, and all other limbs into his shell. "See? Home sweet home!" came his muffled voice from inside.

"I think I could definitely use one of those," sighed Addie. Instead, she sat down on the smooth, gray ground, undid the tie on the lunch sack, and took a nibble of bread, followed by a few sips of lemonade to restore her energy.

Toybox remained standing, gazing around them. Suddenly, he noticed something, "What's that?" He pointed to the horizon. Addie looked.

"Where? It seems empty," she said, peering intently into the distance.

"It's a little speck of something way out there." Toybox

stretched up high to get a better view. "Yep, it's some sort of small house or building," he called down to his friends.

"Maybe whoever is there can tell us how to get to the palace," offered Brother, his head emerging from his shell.

"Well, then we should get moving," said Addie as she rose to her feet.

Toybox, still extended to his high vantage point, looked around the other direction and stated, "I can still see the Land of Sweets from up here! You know it's probably not too late to…"

"*Toybox*!" Addie and Brother interrupted in unison.

"Oh, all right," he pouted and immediately shrunk down to his normal size, falling in behind Addie and Brother as the three resumed their journey.

Chapter Thirteen

ddie and the others were nearing the modest building in the centre of the vast grey plain. As they got closer, the entire area felt drearier and lacked colour entirely. Though very modest, the structure was not run down. And although the architectural style was obscure, it appeared to be a dwelling. It could hardly have contained more than one room, however.

Addie looked around the vacant grounds. "Who do you suppose lives here?"

"Maybe a hermit?" asked Toybox.

As they were gazing at the small structure, however, the procession of Keepers arrived, paused a few seconds, circled the area once, and proceeded directly into the building.

"Whoever it is, they're probably not lonesome, what with the Keepers in there," stated Brother. "It doesn't look like they'd all fit."

"We should introduce ourselves," stated Addie and began

walking toward the door. Upon arrival, she knocked, but, to her surprise, her knocks resounded more like ornate, massive door chimes.

The others had followed closely behind Addie. "Some knock, Your Highness!" commented Toybox.

But there was no answer to Addie's knock. She tried the door. It wasn't locked. She gently pushed it open, and the three cautiously stepped inside.

But what greeted them inside astonished them; it was the same, simple austerity evident on the outside of the building… except that it was *enormous* inside.

"My goodness!" Addie gasped.

"Hey, wait a minute…" puzzled Brother, poking his head back outside to compare.

"Looks like they got an outside a few sizes too small for their inside," Toybox smirked.

There were grand, curved staircases and towering columns, but everything was the same tone of grey and was largely lacking in furnishings or adornment. The slightest sound echoed in the vast emptiness. The Keepers, however, were not in sight.

Presently, though, the Keepers emerged from a pair of tall double doors at the far end of the huge entry hall.

"Oh, here they come!" said Addie, holding up her hand to wave at them, "Please, sirs! We were wondering if you could tell us…"

The hooded figures swiftly moved through the hall and exited the door that Addie and her friends had just entered, paying them little attention.

"Sometimes I wish people had more manners," Brother groused.

In their hurried exit, however, the Keepers left the tall doors ajar, and a flickering warm light could be seen in the dim chamber beyond. The group of travelers edged forward cautiously.

With Addie in the lead, the three cautiously peeked through the doorway into the rear chamber. There, sitting in a plain wooden chair in the centre of the space, was a rumpled figure with his head bowed in his hands. A plain wooden table in front of him held a lighted candlestick, a quill, an inkwell, and a few papers.

Addie managed to muster the courage to offer a greeting, "Hello?"

The figure lifted his gaze to meet hers. He was an older man with long, uncombed grey hair and a similarly bedraggled beard. His clothing was plain, worn, and even a bit tattered. "What is it you wish?" he asked matter-of-factly.

"Excuse me, I…" began Addie. "We are looking for Prince Fedor's palace."

"For what it's worth, you've found it," said the man morosely.

A brief wave of elation went through Addie and her friends. However, the contradiction with their expectations soon set in, and their smiles faded into bewilderment.

"This is…the palace?" asked a perplexed Addie; she then went straight to the matter: "May we see Prince Fedor?"

"I'm afraid not," the man stated with a sigh. "We don't even know if he's alive. No one has seen him in almost two years. "

"Two years?" Her hopes crushed, Addie's eyes moistened as the hope of being reunited with Fedor dimmed. "We've come all this way, and no one knows where he is?" she lamented to Brother.

"Maybe this man doesn't know what he's talking about," Brother whispered to Addie, trying to console her. "Who is he anyway?"

Addie gathered her wits enough to be able to query the man, "Please, sir," she sniffled, "Who exactly might you be?"

The man pulled open a drawer in the table before him, removing a beautiful but tarnished crown and placing it on the table.

Addie gasped, and her eyes widened, "Then you are King Frederick? And…and…Fedor is your son?"

"Yes, my dear. Sorry for the lack of introductions. And who are you?"

Addie was horrified that she might have disrespected the king. Though her knees were quite unsteady, she curtsied and replied, "My name is Addie, Your Majesty…and…and I bring news for you."

King Frederick eyed her suspiciously, "Speak, child."

"I must inform Your Majesty that I was with your son Fedor just three days ago," she announced.

The king had his head bowed, not really prepared for what she said. Soon, however, it began to sink in. "What is this you say?" The king stood up, peering at her intently. "After all this time, tell me why I should now believe you, a small girl, that my son is still alive."

"He..he made me a princess. You…you'd believe a *princess,* wouldn't you?" offered a nervous Addie.

"Nonsense," the king blustered. "He could never—"

"He gave me this," interrupted Addie, holding out her hand to display the signet ring Fedor had gifted her.

The king was so astonished by this that he sank into his chair in disbelief. He then grasped Addie's hand to examine the ring more closely, and his eyes only opened wider. "And this was three days ago?" he asked, looking up at her with excitement building in his voice.

"Yes, Your Majesty."

The king stepped from behind the table, took Addie's hands in his, and began to swing her in a dance, "Then he's *alive,* alive, alive! My son is alive!" he chanted in glee. Addie started to giggle at the king's happiness.

But all of a sudden, he let go of her hands and grabbed her shoulders, "Where did you last see Prince Fedor?" he asked intently.

"At…at my father's theatre in Liverpool," Addie stammered.

"The kingdom of…Liverpool?"

"I suppose so, Your Majesty. Er, the Ruby Palace is there," she offered, trying to be helpful.

The king turned away from Addie as he pondered, "While you were with Fedor, how was he? Was he well?"

"Yes, he was well, Your Majesty…and happy when I met him. He told me that you had sent him on a mission to seek help for your Village of the Blind. But, he also said that his group had been attacked shortly after leaving Ziymia, and he has been trying to return ever since."

"Oh my heavens!" gasped the king, turning toward her again, "The poor boy!" The king thought for a moment. "So then, how did *you* get here, my dear?"

Addie turned a bit glum. She was hoping to get that answer from *him.* "I'm afraid I don't really know, Your Majesty. I remember I fell a long way into the darkness. When I awoke, I found myself here, in Ziymia."

"She's telling the truth, Your Majesty," offered Brother. "We met her just as she awakened."

"These are my friends, Your Majesty," explained Addie. "This is Brother—he's a terrapin—and this is Toybox. Both are your subjects and have helped me a great deal."

Brother bowed with a flourish. Then he poked Toybox, who got the hint and bowed before the king as well.

The king began to pace slowly. "I want to believe your story, but you see I've had so many months of hearing nothing…"

"Your Majesty, you must believe me…it's all true," urged an emotional Addie.

Then the king smiled and admitted, "I do believe you, Princess. I have just been given a report about what you and your friends did in the village of Verbogen and how much you helped all my subjects there. From that, I believe you're a person of your word."

Brother smiled and looked at Addie, "That report must be why the Keepers came here."

"Correct, Brother Terrapin," continued the king, "I now know, Princess Addie, that *you* are the very help I sent my son to find all those months ago. And we are so pleased with the success you have had and the love for the people that you have shown. You are truly worthy to be our princess."

King Frederick raised his eyebrows as a new realization came to him. He approached and addressed Addie solemnly, "Princess, you've already shown how resourceful you can be in solving the problems we have here in Ziymia. Do you think you could return to your country, *find* Fedor, and bring him home to us?"

Brother smiled and tugged on Addie's skirt. She bent down to him, and he whispered a phrase from the Oracle in her ear:

*...Bring home the crown
Restore the throne...*

Addie turned a little pale. Her heart filled with unease at the immense weight of this request and the burden of admitting, even to herself, that she might be the "One to come." In addition, since she didn't know how she got here, there was little hope of discovering how to get back, much less finding Fedor. But she knew that she did have full use of her eyes now. And if she didn't do this, who would? Who else knew more about this land and Liverpool than she did? But she also knew that failure was a real possibility. Why would she risk disappointing the king?

There was a silence as Addie pondered, looking into the king's pleading eyes. Impossible or not, she had to try.

"Your Majesty, it would be an honor to accept such a

mission," Addie assured King Frederick. "But I will need all the help you and your subjects can provide."

"You will have the Keepers at your disposal. Their knowledge will help you when you don't know what to do," offered the King.

"Thank you, Your Majesty. May I bring my friends as well?" Addie asked as she gestured toward Brother and Toybox.

"They escorted you here, and so they are already my trusted allies," the king replied.

Toybox gave Brother an embarrassing hug. Brother had to wiggle himself free.

"Your Majesty, if I may ask," said Addie, "Why is your palace so…plain?"

The king sighed, "My world became utterly empty when Prince Fedor went missing," he explained. "There was no reason for pomp and pageantry for me if there was no one to share it with. So we've kept our palace austere and plain…at least until the prince returns."

"So why didn't you send someone to search for Fedor two years ago?" Addie asked.

"We *did* send out a search party," explained the king. "But, they never came back either. So we sent out another group—and *they* never returned. As king, I could no longer conscience the further loss of our citizens, so since then, we have been waiting."

"I'm so sorry, Your Majesty," said Addie.

"But now you are here, my dear," encouraged the king. "You have come from that world with blessed news and hope for us all."

Just then, the Keepers re-entered the throne room and came to rest, hovering in a semi-circle behind the king. With his most trusted partners now before him, the king stepped forward, raising his voice to announce:

"Tomorrow, with new hope in our hearts, we will commission a Royal Rescue party, led by Princess Addie, to retrieve our beloved Prince Fedor from the world beyond our borders. Preparations for the journey will commence immediately. But, as of today, this place must be transformed into a proper palace, both in preparation for Fedor's return and for the coronation and celebration of our new princess!"

Addie tugged on the king's sleeve and whispered, "Your Majesty, did you just say you're going to rebuild the palace today —in one day?"

He gave her a sly look, "It's easy if you have the proper architect," he smiled, as if there were nothing unusual about the task. "How about it, Brother Terrapin?" he asked Brother.

"What, who, him?!" scoffed Toybox at Brother. "He'd come up with a design that doesn't have a single carousel, swing, or slide. Booooring," he sniffed and folded his arms.

Everyone turned to Brother, who looked down, nervously twiddling his fingers, and then, without looking up, shyly admitted, "As a matter of fact, I *do* have a design in mind that I'm rather partial to, Your Majesty."

"Would it please Princess Addie?" asked the king, turning toward her.

"Oh yes! I'm sure Brother will do a wonderful job," assured Addie. Toybox rolled his eyes jealously.

"Very well," announced the king, pulling a scepter from the same drawer that had housed his crown and extending it to anoint the kneeling Brother, "You, Brother Terrapin, are hereby appointed our royal architect."

"King's pet, King's pet..." taunted Toybox.

"Toybox, behave yourself!" shushed Addie.

"And you, Toybox…" continued the king—causing Toybox to abruptly snap to attention, unprepared for the king's scrutiny, "You are to see that it is done with all good speed so that tomorrow's rescue mission may proceed in earnest."

"But your Kingliness, how can we build it all by ourselves?" objected Toybox.

"All the help you need is waiting just outside," said the king as Addie and her friends gave each other puzzled glances.

Addie, Brother, and Toybox emerged from the front door of the diminutive grey "palace" to be greeted by rank upon rank of small, glowing creatures hovering a few feet off the ground.

Upon assessing the situation, Addie and Brother both exclaimed in dubious unison: "The Idgits?!"

Toybox, conversely, was elated and began applauding. "The Idgits!" he grinned.

Brother took a deep breath. "Don't you worry, Addie. Just leave them to me. You'll soon see a palace like there never was."

"I'm sure of that," Addie replied with one eyebrow raised, unsure whether to be excited or apprehensive.

Brother reached into his shell, drew out a huge roll of blueprints, and marched into the midst of the legions of floating Idgits. Toybox followed just behind Brother, playfully mimicking his stride. Toybox glanced at Addie, who politely covered her mouth to mask her amused smile.

As Brother unfurled the blueprints, the glowing Idgits began to swarm around him, massing over the plans, emitting a melodious purr. After a moment or two of study, they left Brother, broke into several smaller groups, and zipped to their respective positions several yards away.

One group began about a hundred feet in the air, directly above the small grey dwelling. Once each group of Idgits reached their assigned spot, they started swarming furiously, with ever more intense light emanating from each cloud of creatures. As the first swarm descended, the top of an ornate spire appeared. The more the swirling mass of lights descended, the more of the new structure came into existence.

Elsewhere on the site, much the same process was occurring. Various groups of Idgits were swarming to bring different parts of the edifice and its landscaping adornments into being. All of them began at the top and built downward.

Off in a corner of the grounds, one group of Idgits was under Toybox's command; he was lounging in a hammock being rocked by Idgits as another group of Idgits fanned him. Brother broke away from his duties of inspection and strolled over to Addie. He pointed at Toybox.

"Would you just look at him?" Brother chafed in disgust.

"At least he's out of trouble…" Addie offered, shrugging.

"Not in my book, he's not!" Brother, as the chief architect, would have none of it. He stridently marched over to Toybox, shouting at him: "Toybox! Do something with yourself!"

Toybox was jolted from his reverie, leapt from the hammock, and attempted to put on an air of efficiency. "All right, boys, break's over. Time to get back to business," he blustered in a commanding voice, backing up his charade by pretentiously pointing fingers in every direction as if giving instruction.

Brother walked away in disgust, shook his head, threw up his arms, and returned to measuring distances on his drawings.

Addie smiled at her two friends from a distance, sympathizing with each of them in their silly conflict, which only made her smile more. But she knew she would need those smiles in reserve as tomorrow morning would bring the daunting challenges of leading a royal expedition and finding the way to Fedor. As she considered this, Addie's smile faded into an uneasy resolve.

The instrument-adorned Valley of Music where Addie and her friends had romped not so long ago was now strangely silent, bereft of activity. There were no souls to be seen. Only a slight breeze whistled through the monument-sized musical instruments.

But without warning, a rushing, screaming dark wind tore itself through the valley, fragmenting the landscape into black dust that quickly became an ebony slurry, only to vanish altogether a second later. Everything in the musical valley dissolved and was swept away into nothingness.

Chapter Fourteen

Brother and Toybox were at Addie's side as they stood admiring the completed palace.

"At least the outside matches the inside now," Brother boasted. In addition, the palace grounds were no longer grey, but lush gardens, hedges, and statuary.

And, of course, not surprisingly, the overall form of the palace structure itself resembled nothing so much as a huge, ornately adorned crystal and mother-of-pearl tortoise shell with several grand towers extending skyward from its apex.

"I think I understand why you're fond of the design," Addie winked and nudged Brother as she gazed admiringly upon the magnificent structure. "It's glorious!"

"We should commemorate this moment, Your Highness," urged Brother. "Please turn around."

When Addie did so, she discovered a man wearing an artist's smock and a beret, standing beside a foot-wide box mounted on a tripod. There was a glass orb mounted on the front of the box.

"Your Highness, this is Vincent, the royal portraitist," explained Brother.

"Your Highness," bowed Vincent. "Now, if you would, Your Highness, please stand with your friends over there and look at me."

Addie, Toybox, and Brother obliged, shuffling into position and smiling toward the box and Vincent.

"Ready now, hold still," instructed Vincent as he removed the cap from the glass orb for a few seconds and then replaced it. "All right. All done," he said.

Addie looked at Brother. "All done? What happens next? How does this work?"

"Come over here, Your Highness. I show you," coaxed the portraitist.

Addie and Brother approached the box, hardly noticing that Toybox, unable to wait any longer for his explorations, had spun around and dashed into the new palace.

As Addie drew near the magical box, Vincent opened the hinged front panel like a door, revealing the inner workings. "There, you see?" he gestured. Inside the box, Addie observed a swarm of Idgits within the otherwise-empty box, just completing a detailed eight-inch full-colour painting of herself and her friends mounted on a piece of card. Vincent removed the finished work from the box and handed it to her.

Addie was astonished. "It's beautiful! It looks just like us!"

The Idgits swarmed and giggled, proud of their work.

"May I take this?" Addie asked Vincent.

"Yes, please, Princess. We shall make a larger one later."

Addie handed the small treasure to Brother, asking: "Brother, could you take good care of this, please?" Brother nodded and tucked it inside his shell for safekeeping, patting his chest with pride once it was secured.

"Are you ready then, Princess?" asked Brother.

"Ready?" asked Addie.

"…to see the inside of your palace?" clarified Brother, gesturing toward the entrance.

Addie nodded excitedly and grinned.

"This way, then, Your Highness," indicated Brother.

"Thank you, Vincent!" Addie smiled over her shoulder at the illustrious portraitist as she followed Brother, who offered his hand to escort her toward the front entrance.

When they neared the threshold, the doors swung open to reveal that the somber grey emptiness had given way to ornate, crystalline majesty. Addie looked up in rapt wonder at the glistening domed ceiling, which was comprised of ornamented mother-of-pearl. Lush carpets embellished the golden floor, and vivid tapestries depicting idyllic scenes of Ziymia adorned the walls.

High above, Toybox, astride a crystal banister, launched himself down the curving slide, squealing in delight and landing right in front of Addie and Brother. "What do you think, Your Highness?" he breathlessly asked as he alighted, quickly turning to whisper to Brother, "You *have* to try this!"

"It's…it's more beautiful than words can tell!" grinned a joyous Addie as she gazed around.

Brother beamed, "I'm so glad it pleases you, Your Highness." He then glared at Toybox before motioning Addie further into the palace.

They strode along the burgundy entry carpet. On either side

was a line of beautiful glass rocking chairs. Addie noticed as they passed them by that each had a face…and they were alive, chanting as they rocked: "Yes, Your Highness. Yes, Your Highness…"

Addie snickered at all the agreeability. Looking up, she noticed that the stairway curved upward toward some sort of tower. "What's up there?" she asked.

"Why don't we take a look?" urged a grinning Brother.

Addie headed toward the foot of the stairs.

"Er…you can take the stairs if you wish, Your Highness," Brother pointed out. "But I prefer another way. He opened a curtain to reveal a velvet upholstered chaise inside a vertically oriented golden tortoise shell. He, Addie, and Toybox took their seats, and the shell with its passengers rose to the top of the atrium.

Addie couldn't suppress the smile on her face at the revelation of so many marvels as she continuously scanned her gaze around, each new glance bringing fresh wonders.

Arriving at the higher platform, the three stepped out to the observation balcony of the palace's tallest pinnacle. It encircled the tower so that the kingdom could be observed in all directions unobstructed. The companions gazed in amazement at the world below and around them. Addie stood for a few moments, enjoying the gentle breeze wafting across her face, with the world below her silent and at peace.

Brother didn't say a word. He wanted all of them to savor this moment.

"How can I ever thank you for all this, Brother?" Addie asked.

"You don't have to, Your Highness. We are here for your happiness."

She hugged him. "I know I could just live here forever!" she said, wiping a small tear of joy from her eye. But then she firmly reminded both of them—and herself, "I know you remember, though, tomorrow we must go and retrieve Prince Fedor. We *have* to bring him home. The kingdom is depending on us."

Brother solemnly nodded. "You may count on us, Princess."

Toybox was leaning over the rail to look down the two-hundred-foot column. "I wonder how high a ball would bounce from up here…"

"I wouldn't try it, Toybox," Addie answered, "What if it hit King Frederick?" she asked, half laughing.

But as she lifted her eyes again, Addie gave a little gasp. She suddenly noticed something on the horizon, almost hidden in the mist. "Brother, what's that?" She pointed to what appeared to be a huge, dark wall in the distance. It was so immense that its top was lost in the clouds, with its ends fading into the haze on both the left and right. Unaccustomed to such objects, Addie struggled with her new-found eyesight, not quite knowing how to interpret something so large.

"That's the Wall of Knowing," explained Brother.

"The Wall of Knowing?" Addie squinted, "Who's on the other side of it?"

Toybox feigned being insulted, "Whoever it is, *they* don't *want* us."

"You see, Addie," Brother continued, "No Ziymians are allowed beyond that wall. None of us natives can ever go there,"

"…but we don't know if the wall is meant to keep us in or keep them out," added Toybox, giving a contemptuous raspberry toward the wall.

Addie had never even imagined a structure that large before. The sheer size of it was mesmerizing. It certainly showed that separating Ziymia from what lay on the other side was very important to *some*body. And the massive effort of building such a wall indicated there was a danger to the residents of one side or the other. Although the mystery intrigued her, the more she thought about it, the more it made her shiver.

Brother took Addie's hand. "There's something else I want to show you...this way." Although Addie could hardly draw her eyes away from the Wall, Brother led her and Toybox back into the tower to a central cylindrical chamber constructed of cut and polished glass. In the midst of it sat a single massive crystal, some five feet tall, sitting on an ornate pedestal, ringed by a shelf that was a circular map of the kingdom.

"What is it?" Addie asked.

"Rock candy, I hope?" offered Toybox.

"This is your view crystal," said Brother. "It's like a window to things far away. With it, you can watch over all your realm without ever having to leave your palace."

"You mean I can see things that are happening...somewhere else?" she asked.

"Uh huh...try it. Just touch the place you want to see on this map of the land, and wherever you touch, you'll see in the crystal."

Addie touched the map, and the crystal lit up instantly, displaying a landscape somewhere in Ziymia. Addie touched it again, and the Land of Sweets appeared.

"Oh, Brother! Remember this place?" she said.

"Boy I do!" interjected Toybox.

"...and if you want to explore, just walk around the crystal, and you can see in any direction," continued Brother.

Addie circled the crystal as the view within it changed

accordingly. "How marvelous!" she remarked. "Can it show us what's on the other side of the Wall?"

Brother's eyes dropped as he reluctantly had to disappoint her, "I'm afraid not, Your Highness. The crystal doesn't see that far."

Suddenly, a blast of trumpet fanfare echoed throughout the palace.

"Oh, that's the signal," said Brother. "The king is expecting us."

"Well, then, let's not disappoint him!" said Addie with a smile, and she led the group out of the view-crystal chamber.

But no sooner had the three of them left the chamber than the image in the crystal darkened and the black, howling wind mercilessly sliced through the landscape in view. Within seconds, the Land of Sweets was no more.

In order to descend from the tower, Addie and her friends decided to use the staircase—though keeping Toybox off the banister was a challenge that the other two could barely manage. As they descended into the grand entry hall, there was more than the opulence they had previously seen—the hall was now full to the brim with splendidly dressed courtiers, gentlemen, and ladies, all applauding and smiling up at Addie and her companions as they came down the stairs.

When Addie and company reached ground level, the immense double doors at the far end of the hall opened to reveal King Fredrick, now neat and trim in spectacular royal robes, standing on the platform before his throne, smiling and with open arms. An orchestra began a grand fanfare as Addie, Brother, and Toybox approached the throne.

As they drew near the platform, a courtier affixed an ermine-trimmed robe with a long train to Addie's shoulders. Addie tried to protest, "Oh, this is too much. I'm just—"

"Accept it, Your Highness," Brother calmly urged as he touched her hand. "The people need you to do this. They *want* to do this for you."

Addie decided she needed to consent. Yet now that the reality of reigning as a princess was upon her, she never felt so much like a sheltered little girl from Liverpool. Would she be able to live up to the needs and expectations of the people, of the king? Would she be able to make their lives better? Obviously, there were privileges and pageantry to be enjoyed. But there would be solemn responsibilities as well. Was this what it was like to be grown up?

King Frederick stepped to the front of the platform and raised his arms to address the throng as the music subsided. "Ladies and Gentlemen of the realm," he announced in a bold voice, "I am pleased to inform you that word has come to us that our beloved Prince Fedor, missing from us for all these many months, is, in fact, still *alive.*"

The crowd gasped, followed by whispers of amazement and then a burst of enthusiastic applause. King Frederick once again raised his hand to quiet the ovation. He continued, "This information was brought to us personally by a brave and brilliant young lady, who not only aided us in solving the distress in our village of Verbogen…" Spontaneous applause interrupted the king. As the applause subsided, he continued: "…but she was, in fact, personally chosen to be our princess by none other than Prince Fedor himself."

More applause ensued. Addie was smiling but blushed intensely.

"Now we must celebrate with all our hearts this day, for I must also announce that tomorrow, the princess has agreed to lead an expedition back to her former land to locate Prince Fedor and return him here to his home among his beloved people."

Cheers rang out from the crowd.

The king held out his hand, inviting Addie up the marble steps to the throne platform. "And now, good citizens of Ziymia, please join me in welcoming your new Princess Addie of Ziymia!"

The orchestra struck up a regal procession as Addie climbed the steps. As she reached the platform, she found herself in the embrace of King Fredrick's kind arms while applause thundered around them. A courtier presented her with a golden scepter and, as she turned to face the crowd, King Frederick stood behind her, placing an elegant, jeweled tiara upon her head. Addie struggled with all the adulation.

After all, a very short time ago, she was merely a blind girl in Liverpool. Another courtier brought a mirror so that Addie might see herself with her crown and scepter.

Is that really me? she asked herself, for she had never seen a true and full reflection of her image before. She glanced down to her enthusiastic friends Brother and Toybox in the front row, applauding heartily. Her eyes moistened as she found herself wishing with all her heart that Papa could see her at this moment, in all this splendor.

"And now," proclaimed King Frederick, "Let us dance until the stars come out to welcome our new Princess Addie!" The orchestra immediately launched into an elegant waltz. The crowd paired off into dancing couples. Addie noticed Toybox jumping up and down with his arms held out toward her. She looked to the King, and he nodded his approval. She unclipped her royal robe and train—a courtier took it from her shoulders—and she descended the steps into Toybox's waiting arms for the first dance.

It really *was* the first dance as Addie had never danced before —especially with a partner who was a conglomeration of toys— but after watching those around her, Addie felt that she and Toybox managed the task tolerably well.

And beyond the dancing, there was laughter, and new friends, and splendid foods and music that Addie knew would all be cherished in her heart for a very long time.

As the festivities swirled, Addie was enjoying herself so

much that she scarcely noticed that the Keepers had entered the hall and had hurried to circle themselves around the king, convening what appeared to be an urgent conference. From the look on King Frederick's face, it was a solemn meeting. Addie decided that they must be engaging in preparations for tomorrow's rescue expedition, an endeavour that, she had to admit, gave her butterflies.

For now, though, she joined with the members of the court, along with her friends, embracing the merrymaking long into the night.

As morning came to the city of Manchester, Charlie returned from the nearby telegraph office to the hotel room where Fedor was waiting. Fedor stood up and peered at him anxiously. "No, Lad. No response yet. Ezra's a busy man, so don't fret yourself too much. He'll respond to my wire soon."

Fedor wasn't happy to hear this, his mind manufacturing all sorts of dreadful things to explain the evidence.

But Charlie was of little solace. "I'll be off to the pub now, Lad," he proclaimed. The warm weather prompted him to remove his coat and hang it on a hook before stepping outside again. He confirmed his watch and wallet were nestled in his vest and, grabbing his bowler, was out the door.

Fedor sat down on the bed to think. What could be delaying the response from Addie's father? But then, when he looked up, he noticed the corner of some papers peeking out of Charlie's coat on the wall. Fedor's pulse quickened as temptation immediately reared its head. Charlie still hadn't told him much about his business meeting back in Liverpool. Perhaps these documents might shed light on what the future held for them. He took the sheaf of papers from the coat and began going through them. Most were things like hotel receipts. But one was a telegram dated yesterday, the 17th of June:

To Mr. Charles Reynolds,
From: Nicholas Foerster
All agreements in order. Please meet us in London Office with
the boy 27 June. Sail to New York 29 June.

Whatever other meanings this message might convey, it became clear to Fedor that he would soon be on his way to America! That would be a month's long journey across the ocean. It would mean a much greater separation from Addie and far less likelihood that he would ever see her again—even if she was doing well now.

The panic from two nights ago suddenly swelled in his throat again. He could no longer wait for communications to confirm that Addie was all right. He *had* to get to her, Charlie or no Charlie as time was running out.

From his wanderings, Fedor knew where the train station was. He dreaded what Charlie might do if he discovered he had set out on his own. Good Charlie could easily get transformed into an angry and ugly Charlie. But he would have to take that chance. There was one thing that might soften Charlie a bit, however—if he left a note. At least Charlie would know where he was and wouldn't worry—but he would also be able to track him down, though that didn't change the fact that he had to go. Now. Fedor quickly scribbled on a scrap of paper: *Gone to Liverpool* and left it on the table. He collected what belongings he could carry, threw on his cloak, and headed out.

Several minutes later, he stood in front of the ticket counter at the station, examining the schedule. The next train to Liverpool was at 1:00 AM. He examined what was left of his allowance in his pocket—he had nearly a pound. That should be more than enough, he thought.

Making sure his hood was in place, Fedor approached the clerk, keeping his head down. "How much is a ticket to Liverpool?" he asked.

"What class?" asked the clerk, not even looking up.

"Third, please."

"That'll be thirty-five pence."

Fedor placed the coins on the counter, and before he knew it, a ticket was in his hand to take him to his dear Addie once more.

As the Ziymian sun peeked over the horizon, Addie slowly began the process of waking up in her tortoise-shell-shaped four-poster bed. She finally opened her eyes and confirmed that, yes, her eyes were still functional, and that fact alone was a reason for gladness. There were so many splendid things for those eyes to enjoy here. Yet they were nearly superseded by the excitement and anticipation of a journey beginning today that could reunite her with Fedor. She almost dreaded returning to England with all its noise and foul smells but then, having never actually seen it, admitted to herself that she couldn't be certain that it wasn't as beautiful as this place. But what awaited her there, a life without Rachel and a banishment to boarding school, certainly didn't beckon her heart homeward.

A knock came at her door, followed by a chambermaid who announced; "Breakfast, Your Highness." The maid was pushing a rolling cart topped with multiple golden tortoise-shell-shaped covers for the various dishes presented. Addie sat on the side of her bed and the cart was rolled to her. The golden dish covers were removed, presenting Addie with a lavish offering of breakfast sights and smells.

"This is wonderful!" she told the chambermaid.

"I'm glad it pleases Your Highness," the maid smiled. "Is there anything else Your Highness might require at this time?"

"It's all so splendid I don't know how I could ask for more," said Addie.

"When you are breakfasted and dressed," noted the chambermaid, "His Majesty has requested an audience with you as soon as you're available."

Addie's eyebrows raised, "Tell his Majesty I shall see him shortly."

"Yes'm" bowed the chambermaid as she exited the room.

With an urgency to meet with the king, Addie was unable to fully enjoy the sweet and savory delights that had been placed in front of her. Nevertheless, she did her best to do so rapidly.

Following breakfast, she soon discovered the velvet dress with a lace collar that had been laid aside for her. But she noticed her reflection in the dressing table mirror and paused for a moment to marvel at it, turning this way and that as she luxuriated in the newfound wonders of a mirror. "How do you do, Miss Addie?" she curtsied. As she gazed at her image in the mirror, she couldn't help but consider whether all these wonders were solid or whether she would soon wake to find it had all been a dream. But she had slept just a short time ago in that four-poster bed. Does one sleep in one's dream? Or must it always be the other way around? No matter for now; she had appointments to keep.

Upon noticing from her reflection that she was still in her dressing gown, Addie hurriedly put on the velvet dress, and the shiny, buckled shoes that accompanied it, tidied her hair with the silver brush from the dressing table, and prepared to meet the king.

Chapter Fifteen

When Addie arrived in the throne room, Brother, Toybox, a group of Keepers, and King Frederick were already there.

"Good morning, Princess Addie," greeted the king. "Final preparations are almost complete for your journey. You will have a single carriage, supplies, a coachman, two guards, and a contingent of the Keepers. The Keepers have their own transportation. And, of course, Brother Terrapin and Toybox will accompany you." Addie was glad her friends would be along for the adventure. Just their presence made her smile inside.

"You will be taking the same route that Prince Fedor's expedition took when they went missing two years ago," the king continued. "It takes you south, through forest and mountains towards Europe. You will have the best charts and navigation I can provide. And the guardsmen will be well-armed. Are there any questions so far?"

"What shall we do when we encounter a language we don't understand?" asked Addie.

"The Keepers will help keep communications from disruption," promised King Frederick.

"When do we depart, Your Majesty?" asked Brother.

"As soon as the final trunks and cases are loaded on the carriage. If you leave soon, you should be able to make the border by noon and St. Petersburg by nightfall. There, you should be able to gather information, directions, and any additional supplies you might need. Anything else?" the king asked.

The group was silent, absorbing the challenge of the mission. The immense responsibility was beginning to burden Addie. But, no matter the dangers they might face, the prospect of failure was something one didn't even want to think about.

"I want to thank you all for your bravery, dedication, and sacrifice to be a part of this expedition," Frederick emphasized to the group, "The stakes for myself, Prince Fedor, and our country could not be higher. So may I wish success for you all and Godspeed on your journey".

"We won't let you down, Your Majesty," asserted Addie, holding out her hand to the king. Despite this, he couldn't help but scoop her into an embrace, partially so that she wouldn't see his eyes glistening. "I know you'll do well, Princess. Bring our prince home."

"You can count on us, Your Majesty," added Brother.

"What he said," added Toybox.

It wasn't very long before the white and gold carriage was fully laden with its cargo. One of the two guards rode next to the coachman, and the other stood on the rear platform. The members of the expedition said their goodbyes to the contingent of courtiers and citizens who had gathered to see them off, then solemnly boarded the royal coach. Two golden horses with white manes and tails drew the carriage, presenting a handsome image of the land of Ziymia for all who might see it pass.

The sun had just risen high enough to reflect off the mother-of-pearl dome of the palace as King Frederick approached the carriage window for a final sendoff. "I'll be waiting for your messages, Princess Addie," said the king. "Hurry home."

"We'll write every day, Your Majesty," promised Addie as she leaned out the window to wave at the king and the onlookers. She looked around to note that it was a beautiful day for such a sendoff. The only clouds in the sky, though somewhat dark, were far off on the horizon.

The coachman took the reins, and the team of horses set off, heading straight from the palace down the path toward the road. All the passengers leaned out for a final wave. They then settled back into their seats, preparing for the long journey ahead.

"Wait! Stop!" shouted Toybox abruptly. "We've got to go back!"

"What's the matter?" asked a breathless Addie.

"I forgot my tennis racket," Toybox admitted.

Brother rolled his eyes, and Addie poked Toybox sharply in what might have been his ribs.

Before long, the sun got higher in the sky, and the mountains began to get closer as the carriage rumbled down the road. Addie stared out the coach window as she mulled over her memories of Fedor and tried to work out how they might be able to find him. And she cherished how proud Fedor would be of the positive changes in his kingdom that she had helped to initiate. But she looked forward to having him back on the throne.

Brother was struggling to see out his window and found he had to stand on the seat in order to do so. When Addie noticed this, she pulled down a plush pillow from the overhead rack, providing just enough height for Brother to see out comfortably while seated. Toybox occupied his time playing with some of the toys that comprised his body. He was enjoying a spinning whirligig on his arm when Addie's face became puzzled.

"What is that sound?" she asked the group. It was a distant but growing hiss that was rising rapidly. The air smelled of lightning. Out the window to the right, she saw a thin line of darkness at the horizon. But as she continued to peer at the line, it became evident that it was moving, and it was moving at a rate that would soon intersect with their path. "Look! Out there. Do you see that?" she pointed for her companions.

"What is it?" cried Toybox, his voice trembling. By now, the hiss had become an overwhelming roar.

"Coachman, stop!" Addie yelled. The coach pulled up to a halt, but the wave of darkness was still rapidly approaching. "Turn back! Coachman! Turn back!" Addie shouted.

The coachman turned the rig around even though doing so consumed precious seconds. He then brought the team of horses up to a full run as fast as he could manage, even resorting to the whip to help gain speed. Addie looked back to witness a cloud of black dust and darkness enveloping the landscape behind them. Trees, fences, and everything were being torn apart by the howling wind, crumbling into fine black dust and, ultimately, darkness.

The wave of destruction seemed to be pursuing the coach—and getting nearer. A finger of the darkness surged toward the carriage from the right, causing the coachman, already pushing the horses for all they were worth, to swerve in an attempt to avoid the monstrous force. He managed to do so, but in the radical turn, the coach was briefly up on two wheels; its door flew open, and despite Addie desperately trying to hold on to Brother, several cases, along with a frightened Brother, tumbled out to the ground. Addie screamed: "Brother!" but with the roar of the storm, her voice was all but lost in the darkness.

Brother quickly got to his feet and vainly began running after the carriage. Soon, realizing his short legs were no match for the horses, Brother decided to take cover, withdrawing inside his shell to attempt to ride out the oncoming force.

Toybox looked back toward Brother, assessed the situation, and, before Addie realized what was happening, opened the coach door and dove out to attempt a rescue. At the speed of the carriage, all he could do was fall and roll in his exit. Addie watched with horror from the rear coach window.

But Toybox quickly sprang back to his feet and, extending his legs for longer strides, reached Brother before the darkness consumed him. He grabbed the now-compact shell—with Brother inside—and immediately swept off back toward the carriage, much to Addie's great relief.

With his long paces, Toybox managed to catch up in a few seconds, but the speed of the carriage was so rapid that re-boarding was going to be difficult. The guard on the rear plat-form held out his hand toward Toybox, who was running with all his might in pursuit of the speeding coach. Toybox managed to hand Brother over to the guard, who brought him aboard to safety. Addie observed this, her heart pounding, with great solace and delight, through the rear window. She could now allow herself to breathe.

At this moment the roar of the darkness began to diminish. Addie thought the horses must have outrun it. Nevertheless, although the destruction had been done, the ferocity of the storm was, in fact, quickly dying down and began to dissipate. Finally realizing this, Addie called out: "Coachman, you can slow down. Let Toybox catch up."

The coachman did more than that; he pulled over to the side of the road and stopped in order to cool the horses. The coachman and front guard climbed down to tend to the panting team. The rear platform guard stepped to the ground and approached the coach's side window, inquiring if everyone aboard was all right. A frightened Addie and Brother answered in the affirmative as they stepped out of the coach to meet a gasping and winded Toybox. The three clung to each other desperately as

Addie whimpered. "Brother," she wailed, "I can't believe we almost lost you." She hugged him close.

"Yes, but lost me to *what*?" whimpered Brother. "We've never had a storm like that in this land before."

The three, along with the guards and coachman, could do little but stand and stare in silence at the immense and fearsome void behind them. It was hard to know how much had been destroyed because there was simply nothing there but emptiness.

Seemingly from nowhere, the Keepers appeared, circled above the coach briefly, and headed off toward the palace. Toybox tried to flag them down, "Helloooo! What about us? Where are you going? Hey!" But they paid him no mind and soon vanished over a ridge. Toybox sat down on a stone and sulked.

"We await your orders, Your Highness," offered the rear guard to Addie.

"Coachman, is there another way to get to St. Petersburg?" asked Addie.

"None that I know, Your Highness. There was one road. And we don't know what else might have been destroyed."

Addie pondered. How could they abandon their search for Fedor? And yet their only known path to that search had been destroyed. "It seems we have no choice for now," she concluded, "We'll return to the palace and make further plans from there."

King Frederick pounded his fist on the table. "It's not like any storm we've ever seen here!" The king's face was flushed, and his voice was tense, "The Keepers assured me they thought it was limited in its extent. But now substantial areas of our kingdom are destroyed." He addressed the members of the now-returned expedition, including the coachman and guards, along with Addie and her friends. He used the view crystal to highlight the damage done to the kingdom. "Musical Valley…gone! Land of Games…gone!" He turned to the group. "Could someone please suggest a plan?"

The king's frustration and anger were daunting everyone in the room, with few ideas for a way forward coming from anywhere.

"Isn't there a law against creepy black gooey destruction?" asked Toybox.

The king didn't have the patience for Toybox's foolishness, and Brother could see that Frederick was about to erupt and he had to act quickly:

"Your Majesty," Brother began, "We agree that this is more than an ordinary storm. So, we find ourselves in need of an extraordinary solution. At the risk of seeming like a flatterer, Your Majesty, it is well known that the royal decrees issued from your throne have more weight and impact than those of other monarchs."

"That's it. A joint decree, Your Majesty!" chimed in Addie.

"If it is issued by both yourself and Princess Addie, Your Majesty, it cannot be denied, even by a mysterious force," asserted Brother.

Addie leaned down and whispered to Brother, "Is that true?"

Brother shrugged and whispered back, "Royal decrees in Ziymia are more like magic spells in other kingdoms…I hope."

The king was not excited about such a prospect. "I've never seen any *ordinary* storm that would respond to a royal decree, much less one with this much power."

"But who knows what or who is controlling it?" asked Brother, trying to believe it himself. "Perhaps they might even respect a royal decree. Besides, was it not by your royal decree that gravity itself was made optional for holidays and festivals? Your decrees are legendary, Your Majesty."

King Frederick wasn't convinced.

"Your Majesty, at this point, what have we to lose?" Addie pointed out.

This did not make the king any more enthusiastic about the plan. But Addie was right. "Brother Terrapin, draw it up, and I'll sign it," said the king.

"…and I'll put my seal on it," said Addie, holding up her signet ring, mustering a slight hopeful smile.

"Let me know when it's ready," muttered King Frederick bleakly as he left the chamber.

Within a couple of hours, the scroll was prepared and ready for the royal endorsements. When the king was informed of this in his chambers, he requested that the document be brought to him on the observation balcony in the palace's central tower, the highest point in the land. He also requested that Princess Addie and the others join him.

When Addie, Toybox, and Brother arrived on the balcony, King Frederick was waiting for them, flanked by two palace guards and the royal crier. A signing table had been set up with a quill pen, inkwell, candles, and sealing wax. "Are you ready, Princess Addie?" the king asked. She nodded solemnly, where-upon he offered her the quill. Toybox and Brother stood at atten-tion, side by side near the doorway as observers.

Addie stepped up to the table, dipped the pen, and signed the decree. She then handed the pen to King Frederick, who proceeded likewise. They each dripped hot sealing wax in their turn upon the bottom of the document and impressed their respective signet rings, thus sealing the document to be as official as could be accomplished in this kingdom or any other. Once the wax had cooled and solidified, the king rolled the document and handed it to the royal crier. "Crier, do your duty," he ordered softly. The crier took the scroll, stepped to the outer rail, faced the horizon, and began to read in a bold voice:

"Whereas the sovereign kingdom of Ziymia has of late been troubled and attacked by dark forces of unknown origin. And whereas those attacks and their resulting destruction have become intensely troubling to the king, the princess, and the people of Ziymia, we hereby pronounce and decree that the senseless destruction now taking place in this kingdom shall cease immediately and forthwith."

As the echo of the crier's words faded, the only sound was from the slight breeze that whistled through the tower. Each member of the party stood silently, diligently scanning the horizon for any activity or trouble. Only a peaceful kingdom was on display.

The silence broke when Toybox began clapping, "Oh, that was wonderful, Your Majesty, Your Highness! Very official."

"Do you think it did any good, Your Majesty?" asked Addie as the king stroked his chin.

"Perhaps you'd like to check the viewing crystal, Your Majesty?" offered Brother.

The group migrated the few steps to the viewing-crystal chamber. King Frederick touched the circular map beneath the crystal, and a view of somewhere in Ziymia glowed within the crystal. Addie and King Frederick strolled around the display, examining the landscape from every angle. Nothing troubling was in view.

Addie touched another spot on the map, "Let's see somewhere else."

Still, only normalcy reigned. Addie touched another spot; the Land of Toys, where she had first met Toybox, lit up within the crystal. It, too, was peaceful—but only for a moment. The group collectively gasped, and Addie screamed as the all-too-familiar dark wind suddenly enveloped the landscape in view, destroying it utterly in moments. King Frederick had to look away as his kingdom was being attacked once more. He turned and stood with his hands on a nearby table, eyes closed, with his head bowed.

Addie was frantic. "It…it didn't hear us! It must be too far away to hear the decree."

Brother touched several other areas on the map to check them, "…but it's still heading towards us! We need a *messenger*, Your Highness, to reach it before it reaches us."

"Yes!" Toybox spoke up, his eyes focused on Brother, "Someone to tell that…that old *nasty* out there what the royal orders are!"

"Yes!" Brother stared back at Toybox, "Somebody to *bravely* save the kingdom and win her Highness's undying *gratitude*, maybe even a medal…"

That got Toybox's attention. He turned around and enthusiastically raised his hand. "Let *me* go, Your Highness!"

Addie scowled, "Oh, Toybox, it's so dangerous. We'll send the Keepers…"

Toybox rolled his eyes, "What's it gonna do, tear me apart?" With that, all the bits and pieces that comprised his body flew apart briefly and then snapped back together. "Besides, I can get there faster than anyone."

"How?" asked Addie.

"Just watch." Toybox stepped back and transformed into a big spoked wheel, his face at the hub, and rolled around the room rapidly. He then returned to his human-like shape and stood once again before them. "See?" he bragged.

Addie didn't quite know what to say. She hated to see her friend in danger. "Toybox, I can't let you…"

Toybox became serious for once and looked intently at Addie, "Please, Your Highness. A fella can't just have fun *all* the time. I need to do this—for you." Addie was even more speechless. She looked over to King Frederick for his opinion. He hesitated but gave a slight nod, then looked away.

"All right then," Addie conceded as she ceremoniously approached Toybox. "You have your mission, brave Toybox." Brother handed her the rolled parchment. Toybox knelt, and Addie touched each of his shoulders once with the scroll. "You are now our royal emissary."

"Thank you, your Princess-ness. I won't let you down." He took the scroll and tucked it in his "belt."

Brother extended a hand to Toybox, "Godspeed, Toybox."

"Thank you, Brother Terrapin," said Toybox solemnly as he took Brother's hand. As soon as their hands met, however, a rude *honk* came from a squeeze toy in Toybox's hand. Brother scowled at Toybox's inability to be serious, even for a moment. Toybox giggled hysterically, turned into his wheel shape, and quickly rolled off and down the stairs to his mission.

The rest of the group somberly watched him go.

"And to think," Brother said quietly, "…all our lives are in his hands."

Chapter Sixteen

It was evening, and a bearded Dr. Gerard Bartlett sat at Addie's bedside, taking her pulse while Ezra and Rachel looked on, feeling helpless. Bartlett then began packing up his black bag and reached for his hat. He stepped closer to Ezra, "It's not looking good, Ezra. I just want you to be prepared. If she doesn't come out of this soon, well…" He couldn't even finish his own sentence.

As the doctor made his way to the door, Ezra found his only source of solace in the stoic arms of Rachel, who held him close in silence as he softly wept. Though this was certainly a trial of Rachel's faith, it seemed to Ezra an all-out assault on his very being. In that moment, he realized that Rachel's small gesture of kindness and compassion was all he truly possessed.

Addie, King Frederick, and Brother gathered in the view crystal chamber, hoping to glean any results from Toybox's mission. Brother operated the map. Currently, the crystal only displayed peaceful views of the kingdom's many beautiful assets. Brother flipped through them rather quickly. Toybox was not in any of them. Until…

"There he is!" pointed an excited Addie as Brother changed the view to display a serene countryside with a narrow river, gumdrop trees, and lots of wildflowers.

"I don't see him," said the king.

"Step over here, Your Majesty," coaxed Brother. "Now do you see him?"

The king adjusted his point of view slightly. "Ah yes, I can see him now."

"Can we follow him, Brother?" asked Addie.

"I'll do my best, Your Highness," Brother replied, attempting to delicately change map positions enough to keep Toybox in view. He was having some success while the king and Addie circled the crystal, looking for any approaching danger. Toybox had stopped briefly and transformed into his human form to get a drink from the gurgling stream.

"Oh no!" Addie exclaimed. "Look behind him…"

As Toybox finished his drink, he stood up again and transformed back into his spoked-wheel form to continue his journey when he heard—and then witnessed—the all-consuming darkness approaching from his left. The terror of it stunned him for a moment. "Gasp and shiver!" he said to himself and then transformed once again into his two-legged form, clutched the parchment scroll, and steadfastly made his way toward the oncoming darkness. He climbed up the riverbank and then clambered atop a large rock at the top of the bank. The ominous cloud of darkness was approaching his position rapidly from the distance. Despite the increasing wind, Toybox unfurled the scroll and, at the top of his voice, began to shout the decree. This did not take long but seemingly had little to no effect on the approaching storm. The wind was increasing, accompanied by an ever-widening howl.

"It's no use, Toybox!" a tearful Addie yelled—though he could not hear her. "Get out of there!"

But Toybox determined to read it again. *"Whereas the sovereign kingdom of Ziymia…"* he began. The land before him began to break apart, with the wave approaching him rapidly. Toybox was forced to break and run before the onslaught but continued reading even as he was overtaken.

Then a helpless Addie, Brother and the king watched in horror as the dark destruction washed over Toybox, sweeping him away. The crystal's image, too, was overcome with blackness, and its window went completely dark.

Addie mourned, "Poor, poor, brave Toybox!" she wailed. "It was for *nothing!*" She threw herself into the arms of King Frederick, who was nearly as emotional as she was at the continued destruction of his beloved homeland. Diminutive Brother offered what comfort he could by hugging Addie's leg. There was a lengthy silence in the chamber, only broken by the sounds of grief.

"I…I can't believe he's gone," sniffed Addie. "There won't be as many smiles here without him."

"He could be a bother sometimes," muttered Brother, "But there was never a braver or more loyal citizen of Ziymia. I am proud to have called him my friend."

"There has to be an answer here, Princess Addie," King Frederick finally murmured, trying to reassure himself as much as Addie. "We can venerate Toybox, and we will, but unless we can defend the kingdom and solve the problem, his loss will utterly be in vain. Ziymia has been here for hundreds of years, and we've never experienced such a dark enigma as this."

Addie was silent in his arms but was listening nonetheless. Eventually, she began to compose herself. She wiped her eyes and nose with a handkerchief from her pocket, then looked up at the king. He was right. There had to be an answer. "Your Majesty, when did this problem begin? Does anyone know?"

"The Keepers told me that as far as they could tell, it began about four days ago," King Frederick replied.

Four days ago, Addie thought to herself. Why, that was just about the same time she arrived in… Suddenly, all the blood drained out of Addie's face; her knees went weak, and the tears began to flow with a vengeance. She pulled away abruptly from King Frederick, glancing around at the people and places she loved, yet unsure of where to turn or what to do. *Somehow, I brought it here*, she thought. *All the destruction is because of me!*

"Princess, what is it?" asked a puzzled King Frederick, seeing the terror in Addie's eyes.

Brother, too, was concerned for his friend but didn't understand any more than the king, "Your Highness, how may we—?"

At that moment, Addie felt all she could do was run. She dashed down the staircase, across the entry hall, and out the front doors of the palace. She had to get away from the eyes of those she had been hurting, away from their homes and hearths where she might bring more destruction. Her mind was a roiling tumult of fear, dread, regret, sorrow, and utter helplessness. Dashing across the palace grounds, she finally collapsed at the base of a fountain whose spout emanated from the figure of a great fish.

There, she wept bitterly *as if the sounds of the flowing fountain are from my own tears*, she thought.

Back in Liverpool, she had only wanted to say goodbye to Fedor, her friend and confidant. Yet that had brought her to run away from home, and even though it landed her in this wonderful kingdom, it was a kingdom whose destruction she now seemed to be causing. She was the only one who had come from outside Ziymia; the destruction had to have come with her.

Addie sobbed for some minutes, despite the soothing sound of the splashing waters. Soon, however, those sounds began to beckon her into the numbness of sleep—slumber, the only respite she could cling to—till gradually she had left the trouble behind, no matter how transiently.

When, at length, she began to crawl back to consciousness, Addie slowly opened her eyes to once again behold the fountain of the great fish. She stared at it for several moments, not moving.

Presently, she sat up, wide-eyed. "That's it!" she realized. "I'm the Jonah! I brought the curse to this land. And if I brought it, somehow it's up to me to take it away." She recalled the story of the biblical prophet Jonah and how, in a terrible storm, his shipmates determined that a curse on him was the cause of the tempest that threatened to sink their ship. Jonah realized they were right and ultimately convinced the sailors to throw him overboard in order to save their ship.

Addie stood up, straightened her dress, wiped her eyes, and headed back toward the palace. She had begun to formulate what had to be done—what *she* had to do.

· · ·

Stepping slowly inside the front entrance, Addie gazed around wistfully at the splendid new palace, now nearly empty, that had been constructed in her honor. And she recalled the regal celebration that had echoed through these halls mere hours ago. What would those revelers all think now when she told them what she needed to tell? What would they think of her? Would they even believe her?

King Frederick was on his throne, slumped over on one elbow in the same desperate stupor of grief that Addie had embraced. Brother was nearby, hibernating in his shell. The entire palace had taken on the pall and stillness of a mausoleum.

Addie pushed one of the large double doors at the entrance to the throne room open a crack. When she confirmed the king's presence, she opened the door further, wide enough to allow herself entry. The creak of the door's hinge, however, began to rouse King Frederick.

Addie approached the throne. "Your Majesty?" she queried softly.

The king sat himself upright. Addie could see his eyes were dark and reddened. "Yes, Princess," he muttered.

"I have to tell you something." She drew closer and kept her voice low. "You said that the destructive storm came to this land about four days ago."

"Yes…"

"Well, Your Majesty. That was the same time that I myself arrived in Ziymia. I'm certain the two must somehow be related," Addie explained.

"Oh, now don't go blaming yourself, Princess…"

"I'm not, or at least I don't wish to," she said. "But you have to admit it's quite the coincidence."

"Princess, as of now, I don't see anything you or I can do to save this land. If there is help to be had, it must come from beyond the Wall of Knowing. There is knowledge there that we do not have in our land."

Addie thought for a moment, then: "And so it shall be, Your Majesty!" she said, brightening.

The king was listening intently now.

"Only those who are *not* natives of Ziymia may pass beyond the Wall, right?" Addie sought to confirm.

"Yes."

"Well, I'm not a native, Your Majesty!"

Brother was emerging from his shell-based slumber. "She is correct, Your Majesty," he confirmed, stretching himself.

"And so I must be the one to go beyond the Wall for help, Your Majesty," Addie proclaimed. "I brought the darkness, and I shall dispel it, even if only by my leaving this kingdom. And I'll do everything in my power in that world to find and restore Prince Fedor as well."

The king looked at her intently, mulling over the idea and its ramifications. "I cannot let you go, Princess. That would be too big a task for one girl, even a princess." He turned to Brother for help. "Brother Terrapin, talk some sense into her."

Despite the king's request, there was silence. Brother became solemn, staring intently at Addie, a tear welling in his eye. Then he turned to the king. "Your Majesty, I love dear Princess Addie, and I enjoy serving her, and I will gladly serve her to my last breath." He paused, gathering his thoughts. "But it has to be her, Your Majesty. The Oracle; she's the One to come. There is no other way." He bowed his head glumly.

The king was now wide-eyed. "The One to come?" he pondered.

Brother reached into his shell, withdrew the small scroll, and opened it to read:

"...Bring home the crown,
Restore the throne..."

"It's what I must do, Your Majesty," insisted Addie earnestly. The king could see the determination in her eyes. "You know it's the best chance we have." She removed the tiara from her head and humbly returned it to the king. "Please keep this for when I return."

The King remained uneasy about approving such a mission, putting a young girl into danger, despite the arguments that things had to be this way. If it didn't turn out well, it would all be his responsibility for allowing it. And worse, he knew that if anything happened to Addie, he would personally be devastated.

Still, if the Oracle had mentioned it, the outcome was likely already set.

Just then, a contingent of the Keepers silently floated into the throne room and hovered above the platform, not far from the throne.

"Very well, then," stated the king as he turned and approached the lead Keeper. The Keeper held out his lantern, and King Frederick accepted it from him. The king then turned to Addie. "Take this flame. Keep it always with you. For as long as it burns, you are safe. But hurry, time is short; you only have until the flame burns low."

Addie took the lantern, noting how remarkably clear everything around her seemed in its light. "Thank you, Your Majesty. I won't let you down." As she said this, her body began slowly rising skyward! As she watched the group drop away from her, the utter exhilaration of her ascent was only slightly dampened by her sense of apprehension at what lay ahead.

The king continued, shouting as she rose, "The flame protects you, brings you courage, and removes all your burdens and doubts. You can soar as high as you wish and clearly see your way."

Brother waved as Addie continued her ascent, "Hurry back to us, Your Highness!"

A hinged pair of windows opened in the palace ceiling as Addie neared it, allowing her to pass through. "I will, Brother. Take care, Your Majesty!"

The king waved proudly, "May God protect you, Princess!" His words sank into the distance as Addie continued her rise into the sky.

Chapter Seventeen

When she reached an altitude higher than the towers and trees, Addie could clearly see the Wall in the distance. It consumed the entire horizon, its top still obscured by clouds for much of its length. Addie began to experiment with the beacon. She determined that not only was it useful for illumination, but it was also the key to navigation. After a bit of trial and error, she determined that holding the beacon out in front of her with fully extended arms moved her forward at full speed. Bringing it closer to her body caused her forward motion to halt. She could turn left or right by rotating the lantern clockwise or counter-clockwise. If she tilted the lantern's top forward, she discovered that she descended, and by tilting it back, she rose. Within a few minutes, she figured she had complete control of her motion and steadfastly set her course for as rapid a journey to the distant wall as possible. Addie only hoped that she would have as much success once she reached the wall as she'd had in learning to use the lantern. Although she had no idea what to expect there, the fate of the kingdom was at stake; it weighed heavily on her mind.

The sun had gone behind the clouds, and it was nearing the horizon, so daylight was waning. The size of the Wall gave the illusion that it might be nearer than Addie had first thought. But she was soon cured of that misconception. At first, it seemed that no matter how fast she traveled, the Wall remained the same size. In reality it was miles and miles away. She set her speed to the maximum and resolved to enjoy the Ziymian countryside while she could.

A good deal of the country below her seemed devoted to agriculture. She could see farmers and workers below her tending groves of gumdrop trees. The crop seemed to yield all sizes and colours of Fedor's favourite confection. Other fields seemed to be producing crops of shoes, or ribbons, or lace. Interspersed were quaint villages, each of which had its own unique architecture. Some were fairly traditional houses, albeit smaller in size, with lots of colourful shutters and flower boxes. In contrast the structures in other villages might all have conical roofs or construction resembling multi-coloured mushrooms. Addie determined that when she returned, she wanted to visit every one of these beautiful villages and get to know their people.

Before too long, however, the wall got close enough that Addie could begin to detect its texture. Its construction seemed to consist of rough, rectangular stones of various sizes set in random directions, but all with the same dark grey-brown colour. With the dwindling sun, it was getting difficult to perceive the textures, and Addie thought that if it were not for her beacon, she might even collide with the wall in the darkness and injure something.

She was relieved of those thoughts when a small pinprick of light appeared in the centre of the wall straight ahead of her, giving her something toward which to navigate. As she journeyed closer, the point of light slowly revealed itself to be, in reality, two lights—torches, in fact—one on either side of a gateway or opening.

As Addie neared this opening, she became aware that it was a stone archway framing two massive and forbidding wooden doors; their primitive construction and rugged condition implied immense age. Jutting outward from the bottom of the archway was a semicircular stone platform upon which Addie descended and finally touched down; she congratulated herself on an uneventful landing. The thirty-foot-tall doorway seemed to be about halfway up the height of the wall's face, which extended far above and below for heights that made Addie dizzy.

Addie reflected that her former self would never have been brave enough to take on a fearful journey such as this. But in defense of the friends she had made in Ziymia and the land she had come to love, she found herself becoming bolder as she sought to guard those she cared for. And if she was, in fact, the One mentioned in the Oracle, it granted her still more confidence and strength. Besides, she could do no less than what dear, brave Toybox had given his all for.

The doors before her displayed no signs, symbols, or any other markings…only the doors themselves and their large, corroded, dark-metal handles. These handles were nearly out of Addie's reach. *Did that mean they were meant for giants?* she asked herself. Curiously, in such a foreboding wall, there was no sign of a deadbolt, lock, or other securing mechanism in these doors.

Given very little other choice, Addie decided to try the

handle, and the door opened easily; she pushed it inward and cautiously took small steps into the dark chamber on the other side. In the centre of the darkness, some distance away stood a brilliantly ornate brass ticket booth adorned with many electric lights. Beyond that was a less forbidding but still closed doorway labeled "Entrance." The faint sound of a distant calliope echoed through the dark space.

Once Addie was well into the room, the immense wooden door silently closed itself behind her. It seemed she was surely committed to the mission now. She approached the ticket booth, and as she came near, she found it occupied by a somewhat slouchy ticket seller who was an exact duplicate of herself! Addie hesitantly stepped up to the window, peering curiously at her twin. She stood there for a moment, trying to understand.

"May I help you?" asked the ticket seller.

"I…I need to get to the other side of the Wall," said Addie.

"Don't know anything about any wall. Do you want a ticket or not?"

"Ticket for what?" asked Addie.

The ticket seller sighed, took a deep breath, and launched into a memorized—and jaded—spiel that she apparently had given many times:

"See the battle of the century," she began, her voice containing no excitement and her eyes not connecting with Addie or anything else. "The great contest between Otta, Wanna, and Godda. See them battle to the death, the spectacle of a lifetime. Five shows daily…"

Addie was taken aback that Rachel's lesson about managing one's time was now before her as a spectacle. But just as in that lesson, she knew she had to prioritize what was most important at this moment.

"Aren't there any other gates or openings to the other side of the Wall?" she asked insistently.

"No idea. Do you want a ticket or not?"

Addie looked around the sparse room again. Her options were severely limited. "I…suppose so," she conceded.

The ticket seller pulled a ticket from a large roll, "That'll be half your flame, please."

"What?!" Addie demanded. Anger and fear were welling up in her.

"Half your flame. That's the price, Sweetie. Take it or leave it."

Addie looked at the beacon in her hand. The flame was not even as bright as when she had left the palace. Losing more of it would surely reduce her security as her journey proceeded. But what were her other choices?

Rachel had always said that the only way to get beyond one's trials and troubles was to go *through* them.

"All right…I guess," she said finally. It appeared this was her only option to make *any* forward progress.

The ticket seller looked Addie in the eye, blinked her eyes twice, and the flame in Addie's beacon diminished by half, sending a shiver down Addie's back. The seller handed Addie the ticket, and the doorway beyond opened of its own accord. Addie wondered what she had just done.

She stepped through the doorway, and as she tentatively strode down a darkened corridor, the muffled rumblings of a distant crowd grew louder up ahead. The light at the end of the passage beckoned Addie with a combined call of both curiosity and dread.

The corridor gave way to reveal that Addie was in a dimly lit arena, its sides lined with grandstands full to overflowing with familiar hooded figures: the Keepers. They murmured to each other in restless anticipation. Addie herself stood in the aisle, waiting to see what would happen.

In the centre of the arena was a lighted platform, lit from above, on which stood three strange-looking two-legged creatures with no arms and no shoulders, each about two feet high and each a different bright colour. They all stood restlessly, facing a large grandfather clock in their midst.

Suddenly, the clock gave forth a single, deeply resonant chime, larger and louder than it seemed capable of. As if that were a signal, the Keepers in the stands all reached up in unison to lower their hoods. To Addie's amazement, every one of them was a precise and silent duplicate of her, down to the hair ribbons! Her natural curiosity began to turn into real unease.

Why were they all *her*? Addie's heart began to race as she struggled to make sense of this place.

All the Keepers bent forward in unison to retrieve a cup-sized container filled with small round objects from the holders in front of their seats.

The clock struck again—another single chime.

All at once, the three colourful creatures on the platform began charging and devouring the massive timepiece in their midst. The throng of "Addies" began to cheer wildly; many of them began throwing single, round objects from the cups in their hands onto the platform.

One of the hooded Addies approached and silently offered Addie herself a container of the small spheres. When she examined it further, she discovered that the objects were a mixture of glass marbles and multi-coloured gumdrops. "No, thank you," she said, holding up her palm to refuse. "Gumdrops are Prince

Fedor's favourite. We wouldn't want to waste them." The hooded Addie stared blankly at Addie for a moment, then returned to the stands.

As each of the creatures on the platform consumed part of the clock—whose total mass was larger than all three creatures combined—the creatures' sizes enlarged accordingly. With the quantity of marbles and gumdrops accumulating on the platform, sometimes the creatures would trip and tumble from the marbles; sometimes they would squash a gumdrop, adhering them to the floor just long enough for their competitors to gain an advantage in the race to devour the clock.

Addie looked at the crowd; somehow, the arena didn't seem as full as it did a moment ago. The clock struck another single chime.

The creatures continued their feasting on the clock until, before Addie knew it, the timepiece was gone entirely. A roar of cheers erupted from the crowd. Each of the three creatures was now somewhat larger, though they were of unequal size. All three turned outward to the crowd and bowed in unison. The crowd applauded enthusiastically.

The creatures turned back toward where the clock had once stood, paused for a beat, and then set about merrily consuming one another! The larger of them seemed to have an advantage. But their feasting was bloodless—the creatures' insides were like taffy. They began a high-pitched giggling and seemed to enjoy being consumed so much that Addie couldn't help but giggle at the spectacle herself.

As laughter escaped from her mouth, the crowd and the creatures immediately turned to stare at her. All action and sound suddenly ceased.

"It's all right," an embarrassed and blushing Addie offered. "Please proceed."

Instantly, the arena snapped back into its raucous and rowdy contest. But as Addie looked around, there was definitely a large fraction of the throng of robed Addies now missing.

Only two of the creatures remained on the platform. They circled each other for a moment, and then the larger one set upon the smaller—which burst out in laughter—and began delirious consumption.

Now, the crowd had diminished to only a couple of dozen duplicate Addies, and the cheering was reduced accordingly.

As the large creature completed its consumption of the smaller, Addie looked back to see that the audience had vanished altogether. When she returned her gaze to the platform to see what the victorious creature would do next, she found that it, too, was gone.

Addie now found herself in a vacant arena. She checked her beacon. Somehow, the flame looked even dimmer than before. Her time grew short, and she pondered what to do next.

Looking around, Addie spied an unassuming but inviting door on the opposite side of the empty arena. So, she began to make her way toward the door through a maze of overturned chairs, discarded gumdrop cups, and scattered marbles.

Without a doubt, these events were unlike anything she had experienced before. But no matter how nonsensical things seemed, she knew she had to get through. Somehow, some way, there had to be a passage to the other side of the Wall.

As Addie approached the door ahead, a faint warm glow appeared on the other side of its pebbled glass window, indicating there might be someone within. The closer she got, the brighter the glow became.

She pushed the door open and found herself in a plush and comfortable office with Victorian decor. Leather-and-gold bound books lined the walls. There were a couple of leather chairs and a massive desk of polished dark wood. Seated at the desk, illuminated by the soft light of a kerosene lamp, sat yet another duplicate Addie. However, this one was not of flesh and blood, but rather some sort of mechanical representation, complete with rivets and hinges. She/it moved gently and gracefully.

The mechanical Addie looked up to greet the real one. It spoke with an artificial but soothing tone and made smooth, subtle motions.

"Ah! Come in. Sit down. I offer you joy. Won't you have a warm cup of chocolate?" asked the automaton. Despite its gentle manner, the mechanical Addie made the real Addie feel unsettled. Was this what she would become if she were to remain here?

"Thank you, but I need to get to the other side of the Wall. Could you perhaps…and why do you look like me?"

"You're safe here," cooed the automaton. "Relax a while."

"The kingdom is in danger," Addie insisted, "I must get help from the other side of the Wall."

"No one cares about you there…It's dark and full of despair. Come…stay…" encouraged the automaton.

"Prince Fedor is *depending* on me!" Addie persisted.

"You are welcome here. Why would you want all that unhappiness?" asked the mechanical Addie.

Addie thought for a moment, remembering something Rachel had said:

"…if there were no such thing as sadness, how would you know happiness when it came along?"

"Here," offered the automaton, "Perhaps this will make you happy." It gestured toward a ten-inch tall decorative wooden box with an eight-inch opening sitting on the desk. The sound of a music box began to play, and out of the box's opening came a small mechanical ballerina and her accompanying prince. They proceeded to perform a perfect *pas de deux*.

The tiny mechanical wonders enthralled Addie as she imagined the dancers could be herself and Fedor. Their movements were graceful and lovely. Addie sat down in one of the leather chairs to observe the miniature show as it unfolded and quickly became lost in reverie.

Addie had never fully experienced ballet before. When ballet dancers had performed at Papa's theatre, all she knew of it was that their toe shoes made lots of clacking noise on the wooden stage floor. She never knew just how beautiful their dancing could be.

"Come, have a warm cup of chocolate," the automaton urged again as it poured lovely-smelling liquid into a porcelain cup with a gold-rimmed saucer. "Here, let me take that heavy lantern…" The automaton reached for the beacon, and Addie instantly realized the danger she was in.

She clutched the lantern tightly and bolted for the door. Even as she exited the office, she could hear the Mechanical Addie continue its soothing droning:

"Come, sit down. Relax a while…"

Though Addie left the office by the same door she had entered, she now found herself in an unfamiliar space. Whereas when she arrived, it was a short walk from the arena to the automaton's office door, now, upon exiting, she found that there was no longer an arena but a very long corridor to her left and right that ran far into the darkness, beyond the reach of her beacon. Its walls were covered with faded wallpaper, and its floor was a worn floral carpet.

Addie pondered a moment, trying to decide which direction she should take. She didn't get a chance to think about it for long, however, as the mechanical Addie soon appeared in the same doorway she had just exited. The unnatural creature paused.

"Here, let me take that for you. Won't you stay a moment?" intoned the automaton. It then began to approach Addie, forcing her to choose a direction and run.

Addie couldn't see terribly far into the darkness ahead of her with the decreasing light from her lantern. Nevertheless, she ran at full speed to escape the automaton. Fortunately, it didn't take a lot to outrun the ponderous creature. Addie paused to take a breath and glanced behind her. There was no sign of the mechanical Addie.

Turning forward again, she discovered, to her surprise, Toybox standing in the corridor just ahead. Addie was immediately filled with cheer, "Toybox! You're all right! You can't imagine how glad I am to see you."

But Toybox stood motionless with an uncharacteristically solemn look on his face. He said nothing for a few seconds. Then he looked into Addie's eyes. "Addie, it's time to go home," he said with little emotion.

Addie stepped toward him. "What do you mean? I'm *trying* to get home, Toybox! Toybox?"

He didn't move but, to her dismay, began slowly fading from view. Before long, he was gone. What seemed like a joyful reunion had just evaporated into more abandonment and bitter solitude. Her throat began to tighten. What had she just been telling herself about her newfound boldness to protect the ones she cared for? Right now, she didn't feel very bold at all.

But shortly, the whirring, thumping of the automaton's strides became audible in the distance, growing steadily. Even as she struggled to hold back her tears, Addie immediately resumed running as fast as she could manage.

Before long, however, she reached the limit of how far she could run—the end of the corridor suddenly confronted her. It was a wall, nearly featureless save for the same wallpaper that lined the rest of the windowless and doorless passageway.

"Oh no!" she cried, her heart pounding. Already perspiring from her running, she began to sweat even more at the sudden stress of uncertainty. "I knew I should've gone the other direction." She tried to fight the overwhelming sense that she had blundered into a trap, but a trap set by whom?

Addie held out her lantern to examine the hallway for openings or further turns. But it was indeed a dead end. Again, she glanced behind her, peering into the distant darkness. Though it was not yet in sight, Addie could hear the *thump, thump, thump* of the mechanical Addie approaching.

She turned back to the barrier before her, brought the beacon closer to examine the wall, and reached out with her hand to feel the surface for any clues of potential passage. To Addie's amazement, as her hand neared the wall, she felt nothing whatsoever, for her hand had penetrated right through the wall! Looking back over her shoulder toward the sound of the approaching creature, she knew she had no other choice and, closing her eyes, stepped all the way through the ethereal barrier.

When she opened her eyes, Addie found herself in a dark, dank, cylindrical pit constructed of randomly shaped stones on the walls and floor. It was a few yards across, deep enough—and the wall too slippery—to be able to climb out. Her footsteps resonated strangely in the round chamber, and the musty scents of dampness filled her head. She searched the wall throughout its perimeter but found no hint of the long corridor or the mechanical Addie she had left behind. She even attempted to pass back through the wall but discovered that the stones were quite solid now.

She looked upward again at the blackness above her and realized all at once that she had the means of escape in her grasp! It was her beacon, after all, that had allowed her to soar over many miles of landscape to arrive at the Wall. It should certainly lift her out of this pit.

She raised the lantern to examine it and found the feeble flame discouraging. Nevertheless, she held the lantern out in front of her and gently tilted it back toward her, the motion she knew would cause her to rise.

Nothing. And after several attempts, it soon became clear that nothing was *going* to happen. She surmised that the flame was simply too weak now to lift her, a thought that itself was certainly not uplifting. Addie sank against the cold stone wall, crushed in bitter disappointment.

Chapter Eighteen

s Addie felt the cold solidity of the cylindrical pit's stones, snickers of cruel laughter erupted from the darkness at her futile attempt to escape.

Startled, Addie stepped back from the stony surface, looking around for the source of the laughter. All at once, she realized that the stones were alive—vague, disturbing faces were visible, embossed on the stones that made up the chamber walls as if they were the audience to some coliseum spectacle. Horrified, Addie attempted to get a safe distance from them, only to discover that the stony faces were all around her. She held up her diminished beacon to examine her observers as they continued their cold laughter and muttering chatter.

"Ooh, looks like this is the end of it for her!" cackled one of the stony faces, followed by giggles from the others.

"How do I get out of here?" Addie demanded. "I have to get to the other side of the Wall, and my lantern is getting dim."

Only snickers came from the stones.

"Zimiya is in danger! Look, can you get me *out* of here?" Addie asked impatiently.

"Why would we do that, Dearie? You're the most *fascinating* thing to come along in some time." The other stones cast their agreement with "Uh huh," "Oh yes," "Quite so," and "Fascinating."

"Oh, fascinating, am I?" replied a frustrated Addie. She had to think of something. She thought back to all the stories Rachel had read to her as a child. An idea came: "I'll tell you what," she said, "I'll ask you a riddle, and if you can't answer it, you must get me out of here and send me on my way."

The stones tittered with excitement, "Oh, riddles! Yes, let's play! You go right ahead."

"You'll let me go if you can't guess it?" insisted a suspicious Addie.

"Oh yes. Yes indeed. Release you certainly," was the chattery reply.

"Very well, then," Addie said, scratching her head, perusing in her mind all the riddles Rachel had taught her. Then the very one came to her, and she smiled briefly to herself, then became very stern:

"Until I am measured, I am not known. Yet how you do miss me when I have flown! What am I?"

The stones instantly erupted in laughter, which carried on for some seconds until one of the stones spoke up, "Why, that's an easy one, Dearie! It's *Time,* of course. The answer is *Time*." The stones murmured loudly with derision.

Addie was crestfallen. She felt foolish. Worse yet, she felt like a helpless child. Any hint of being brave seemed long gone.

The stones continued babbling and whispering all around her. "All right, our turn, our turn!" piped up a stone from behind Addie. She reluctantly turned to face her adversary.

"If I guess it, will you please let me go?"

"Oh, you'll be out of here, certain enough," the stone replied confidently, its neighbors tittering under their breath.

Suddenly, a ticking clock, with only a second hand, appeared on the wall.

"You have ten seconds," said the stone, "Here is your riddle:

Feed me and I live. Give me drink and I die. What am I?"

Addie scowled, muttering to herself, "I should know this one."

"Give up, Dearie?" The clock ticked down the seconds: Eight, seven, six…

"No, wait, wait. I'll get it…'give me a drink and I die'… hmm." With one second remaining it came to Addie. "I've got it! It's *Fire*. The answer is *Fire*!"

The stone smiled slyly, "Oooh, she chose fire!" All the other stones nodded in agreement.

Another stone across the way added, "Happy to oblige, Dearie!"

All the stones began to cackle as the floor of the chamber erupted into a searing sea of flames. A terrified Addie desperately began searching for a means to escape the scorching heat. "Help! Somebody help me!" she wailed. But every stone in every direction only taunted and laughed at her. The flames began small but quickly grew to lick at her knees, then her arms. Addie desperately wanted, *needed* to scream, but her voice seized in her throat.

Beads of sweat covered the forehead of a pale but silent Addie as she lay motionless in her bed, with Ezra at her side. He touched Addie's face, and his eyes widened.

"She's burning with fever, Rachel. What can we do?" he pleaded.

"The doctor will be back soon," said Rachel as she stepped nearer the bed. "Right now we have to cool her off. Uncover her."

Ezra pulled the bedclothes down to the foot of the bed.

"Now, hand me that towel," asked Rachel, and Ezra took it from the side table.

Rachel took the hand towel to the nearby washbasin and soaked it with water. She then wrung it out and brought it to the bedside, folding it and placing it on Addie's forehead. Rachel then sat down, taking up the vigil at her side, as Ezra stepped into the sitting room two rooms away.

Ezra leaned up against the wall, nearly collapsing under the burden of dread for his daughter, his reddened eyes turned toward the ceiling.

"Lord…you know I'm not one for praying. Matter of fact, this is probably the first time we've spoken…and…I wouldn't be asking you for anything if it were just for me. I know I…" Ezra choked back the tears. "But Lord, if you could just…see your way to help my Addie…please take care of her, Lord…please…" He sobbed silently to himself.

In the nearby bedchamber, Rachel wiped Addie's face with

the dampened towel, refolded it, and placed it once again on Addie's forehead. She then took Addie's hand, stroked it gently, and began to softly sing her a lullaby,

"Hush, little Addie, don't say a word, Rachel's gonna buy you a mockingbird..."

The flames engulfing Addie in the stony pit began to subside as the faint echo of Rachel's song reverberated off into the distance. Within a few moments, Addie was once again alone in silent darkness. She peered around into the void, "Rachel?" But silence was the only reply.

The stony wall of faces had vanished, leaving only darkness. Addie looked at her beacon. Its flame was burning very low. But as she gazed at it, some of the brightness returned. That gave her some hope, for events were certainly not going as she'd like. She had no idea what to do next.

But, just as the realization of her solitude began to catch in her throat, a low thumping sound was heard off in the distance. Addie held her beacon high to try to penetrate the gloom. The sound grew closer until finally, just on the edge of visibility, Addie perceived the source of the rumbling—it was yet another duplicate Addie, but this one was twelve feet tall.

The oversized Addie halted when she came near the real one. They looked at each other for a moment.

Addie tentatively offered a greeting, "H-hello?"

Big Addie tersely responded, "Hello."

"You're...me?" said Addie.

"Oh no; you're *me*," corrected big Addie.

"Why are you so big?" asked Addie.

The big Addie looked down at Addie and put her hands on her hips, "You grew up."

"I always wanted to grow up, of course, but not like *that…*" responded Addie.

The big Addie shrugged. "Childhood does have its advantages," she opined, "…I wouldn't give them up if I were you… and I *am* you. And what makes you think growing up is something you wanna do, anyway?"

Addie was frustrated. "You're talking nonsense! I *have* to grow up…"

The giant Addie looked at her skeptically.

"I have to grow up so I can be *useful*," Addie offered, trying to convince herself.

"Hey, do you want to play some jump rope?" Big Addie pulled a rope from her skirt pocket and began skipping it. Her tremendous bulk began causing near-earthquake conditions.

Addie changed the subject. "Why does everyone here look like me?" she shouted over the din of thumping and skipping.

Big Addie paused and looked back over her shoulder at Addie, "Rachel always said you're your own worst enemy." Her jumping resumed.

Addie fumed, "Even if Rachel *did* say that, I must now get to the other side of the Wall. I—*we* cannot fail Prince Fedor!" Addie proclaimed, her voice starting to crack.

Big Addie kept jumping, but now she added a traditional rope jumping chant:

"Addie an' Fedor sittin' in a tree, K-I-S-S-I-N-G." The large creature laughed brutishly but suddenly halted her jumping as a thought entered her head.

"Oh, excuse me. Did you want to play too? Here." She tossed Addie a big-Addie-sized jump rope of her own.

"Oh, no, thank you. As a princess, I need to give up childish…" Addie began.

The massive rope landed in Addie's face, fiendishly wrapping itself around her throat. Utter panic seized her. The big Addie continued her earth-shaking jumping, oblivious to the gasps and cries of the smaller Addie. But shortly, she changed her jumping pattern and, along with it, her chant:

"Brave fire and ice,
And then be gone.
Brave fire and ice,
And then be gone…"

Addie heard the familiar Oracle's words but had no chance to think about them, frantically struggling with the ever-tightening rope. She pulled at it with her hands and managed to gasp out a few words, "Please, can you help me…I'm caught…" But the large Addie paid her no notice and thumped off into the darkness. *If growing up means treating people like this*, she thought, *I want nothing to do with it*. As the rope continued to tighten around Addie's throat, she struggled ever more desperately, gasping, wheezing…

Fedor had been sitting in the train station for several hours, and it was getting dark. When he closed his eyes he felt even more dread for Addie. He didn't know how or why, but somehow he sensed her pain and struggle.

He also knew Charlie would be upset with him, but he didn't know what else he could do. And now the feelings he was getting made him even more resolute that he was doing the right thing. He knew, though, that he had responsibilities to Charlie and his employers. But somehow, he also knew Addie needed him—and he hated the thought that, on some level, he might even be the cause of her distress.

Suddenly, Fedor spied a familiar figure hurrying through the station. It was Charlie. Fedor closed his eyes with dismay. He wanted to hide, but it was too late, Charlie had spotted him and was rushing over. Fedor's heart quickened. As Charlie approached, Fedor, hands shaking, started backing cautiously away. "Please, Charlie, I can explain."

"It's all right, Lad, it's all right," assured an agitated and out-of-breath Charlie, thrusting a piece of paper in front of Fedor—it was the telegram they had been anticipating. Fedor looked at the paper and grew somber. Amazingly, Charlie wasn't angry. "You were right, Lad. I don't know how. But we need to go. The hotel is gonna hold our gear. I'll get the tickets."

Fedor continued to stare at the telegram. His fear of Charlie had mercifully subsided but was quickly replaced with an even more burdensome fear for Addie. The cryptic words of the telegram only served to intensify his urgent need to be at her side.

Chapter Nineteen

A bitterly cold wind began to blow, bringing with it glinting specks of frost as Addie struggled with the jump rope at her throat.

The world around Addie was quickly becoming a dark world of ice. Though otherwise beautiful, the shimmering crystalline masses were no comfort to a choking, gasping, half-frozen Addie. Soon, the very rope that tightened around her neck had become pure, solid ice. The words came back to her:

"Brave fire and ice
And then be gone."

Was this to be it, then? She thought, *Choking and freezing to death in the middle of who knows where?* Would Fedor—or Papa even know what had happened to her? But that was unthinkable.

Addie determined that, with all that was in her power, this was *not* going to be the end. She would struggle with all she had to overcome this. She gave one last desperate push to free herself.

Suddenly, the rope of ice shattered into a thousand glassy, icy slivers, instantly relieving and releasing a much-weakened Addie, who crumbled to the ground to catch her breath.

Nearby lay her beacon. She crawled to re-claim it with trembling hands. The flame was growing terribly dim as Addie shuddered in the freezing cold.

With Rachel at her side, Addie's body was quiet, her breathing had become wheezing, labored, and weak. She was no longer sweating, but she was pale. Rachel took her hand and reacted with surprise. "Ezra, she's like ice now!" She turned to Dr. Bartlett, who had just entered and was removing his coat. "Doctor?"

As Bartlett stepped over to examine Addie, she began to shiver. He only needed to touch Addie's forehead briefly, "More blankets. We need to cover her with everything warm we can come up with."

Ezra and Rachel both joined in, pulling blankets from nearby drawers and shelves. They covered Addie with several layers, tucking her in as tightly as possible.

Having accomplished that, there was little the doctor, Ezra, and Rachel could do but step back and hope.

"I've done about all I can do, Ezra," Dr. Bartlett remarked soberly, using a handkerchief to clean his glasses. "You may want to send for Pastor Fisher."

With those words, even the iron faithfulness of Rachel was shaken; she collapsed in a chair, weeping.

Ezra approached Addie and sat by her side, taking her hand in his own. "Addie," he said softly. He loved saying her name, even through tears. "Addie, Sweetheart, it's Papa. Come back to us, Sweetheart. Addie…Addie…"

Hearing her name echoing throughout what had now become a land of ice, Addie sat up and listened to the familiar voice coming from the dark sky: "Addie?…Addie?"

"Papa?" Addie cried, blinking back the tears, "Papa, I'm here! I'm trying to get back to you, Papa." But the beloved voice faded. Addie's heart sank once again.

Clutching her beacon, a shivering Addie looked about at her surroundings. She found herself in a severe landscape comprising jutting masses of ice crystals. Nowhere was there a hint of warmth or shelter from the biting wind. The challenge of navigating her journey had now given way to seeking means of mere survival.

Addie tried to warm her hands before the dwindling flame in her lantern. As she did so, the wind calmed a bit.

But when she focused on trying to warm herself, Addie failed to note that behind her approached the lumbering twelve-foot Addie.

When the big Addie's footfall caused a loud crunching, Addie turned to discover the looming creature standing right over her, also shivering. It spoke in a low, monstrous tone:

"Ooh! You have fire. Give *me* fire!" The giant Addie started to reach for Addie's beacon.

No sooner had she spoken, however, but a violent shudder convulsed the big Addie's body, distracting the creature momentarily. The small Addie cowered in terror but realized something with her immense double was not right. She backed away.

When again the big Addie extended her arm to reach for the beacon, another tremor gripped her. She reared back and, before Addie's eyes, transformed in a series of lurches into a monstrous crystalline Addie of ice, its glowing red eyes the only warm colours in the frigid environment. Suddenly, the joys of the land of Ziymia, those of music, sweets, games, palaces, and dear friends, all seemed so long ago and far away. Yet they still fondly beckoned from her memory—but she knew she couldn't dwell on the past, no matter how pleasant. She had to focus on *surviving*, for she had to do at least that in order to get through the Wall.

Transfixed by the dreadful spectacle of the Ice Addie's transformation, the small Addie soon realized that it would be wise to steer clear of this creature.

Just as the newly formed Ice Addie was coming around to gain its bearings, Addie grabbed her beacon and began to run. The sudden movement caught the eye of the Ice Addie, prompting it to begin pursuit.

Addie took a turn round a massive ice formation, losing the slower-moving Ice Addie at least temporarily from view. She paused to determine her next move. There seemed to be little chance of the environment becoming any less hostile. She spotted an outcropping of ice crystals in a crevice at the base of the large ice hill and decided to take shelter while hiding from the ice creature.

Addie crouched in a small pocket of space surrounded by low, quartz-like ice spires, drawing her body and limbs around the beacon, not only to absorb whatever warmth was to be had, but to conceal its tell-tale glow from her pursuer. The falling snowflakes began to increase in numbers. Addie knew this would reduce visibility and help to mask her hiding place, but it could also provide a fluffy insulating layer as she struggled to preserve every hint of warmth.

She suddenly noticed the ice creature in the distance, largely obscured by a haze of falling snow, with its back toward her. But it was in a different direction than she expected. Was she disoriented? Was there another ice creature? As she peered at it moving around, she came to realize it wasn't the ice creature she was seeing but its reflection on a vast wall of ice.

But if she could see the creature, that meant it could also see her in her hiding spot—at least in the reflection. It still hadn't spotted her, but she had to be prepared. Addie continued examining the environment and discovered that, at the foot of that reflective wall of ice, was a sheer drop—an open chasm. Perhaps she could lure the creature into the drop by making it think that her reflection was the real Addie.

The creature was still trudging about, searching for Addie. It turned slightly toward her. Addie realized this was her opportunity. Shouting, she took out her beacon and waved it toward the reflecting ice wall in an attempt to attract the creature's attention. Before long, the ice creature dutifully responded. With its eye captured by the moving beacon, it immediately began moving rapidly toward Addie's reflective trap.

But to Addie's horror, the creature stopped just short of the precipice. Even worse, from that position, the creature could see both Addie's reflection and Addie herself in her hiding place. The snowfall was beginning to clear slightly, but the creature had not yet spotted Addie. It roared menacingly as it surveyed the area.

Addie cowered, closing her eyes against the creature's

horrific, soul-chilling cry, uncertain whether her own trembling stemmed from the cold or sheer dread.

The Ice Addie at last spotted her, emitted a low snarl, and rushed toward her refuge spot.

Addie was forced to make a break for it. She clutched her beacon and fled in terror back the way she came, closely followed by the Ice Addie.

A narrow passage at the foot of two huge ice mounds presented itself, and Addie scurried along the narrow path, dodging as best she could the sharp crystals that were jutting out everywhere. The Ice Addie didn't bother with such niceties; it crushed right through any ice formations that might lie in its way.

Addie was growing weary from the chase. Though her breathing was reduced to gasps, she knew she could not rest even for a second, for the huge creature was mere moments behind.

Before she knew it, Addie emerged from the narrow passage-way, only to find herself on a ledge overlooking a broad, gaping ravine. She was forced to halt abruptly; any further progress would plunge her hundreds of feet straight down onto the jagged crystals.

She anxiously searched for an alternate route to the left or right, but none could be found.

The Ice Addie was approaching quickly. When it caught sight of Addie, it paused briefly a few yards away as it realized its prey's predicament. Smiling as much as an ice monster could smile, it demanded: "Give, fire."

Addie clutched her beacon tighter than ever. The creature turned to gesture toward a nearby wall of ice. As it did so, a warm glow grew inside the transparent mass to reveal a startled and fearful Brother suspended in the ice! Embedded in the icy wall, Brother could not move, but his eyes looked toward Addie pleadingly.

The ice creature repeated: "Give, fire."

Addie was skeptical, "That can't really be Brother," she shouted at the ice creature. "He can't go beyond Ziymia!"

The creature smiled again and replied, "You...certain?"

Addie was not certain of anything at this point. When she looked out again into the abyss, her eye was caught by a small glint of colour in the vast, threatening desert of ice. As she looked closer, she realized that it was a small cluster of golden Daffodils atop a pillar of ice not far below. It was Pastor Fisher's illustration of faith from so long ago! As she looked at her beacon, the flame grew distinctly brighter.

The ice creature stood by impatiently, shifting its weight from one foot to the other while Addie mulled the options. The flame and the flowers gave her much-needed courage.

Addie demanded: "If I give you the flame, you'll set Brother free?"

The ice creature slowly began moving toward Addie, one hulking, crunching step at a time.

Addie was paralyzed with fright. "No! No, please!" she screamed.

The Ice Addie paid no heed, drawing ever closer as Addie was forced to the brink of the vast abyss.

Now close enough to reach Addie, the creature slowly extended its massive arm towards her beacon. "Fire..." it growled single-mindedly.

Addie now saw herself and her beacon reflected multiple times in the icy creature's facets as it gradually closed in to ensnare her.

From somewhere, the instruction King Frederick had given for Addie's beacon came back to her:

"The flame protects you, brings you courage, and removes all your burdens and doubts."

These near-forgotten words offered her strength—but how could she actually make use of their promises? The words were inspiring, but what she so direly needed was action as the creature's outreaching hands came near.

Now, completely out of options, and in a final desperate gesture, Addie whirled and flung the beacon with all her might into the stark red eyes of the Ice Addie and, having done so, collapsed to her knees in whimpering, trembling defiance.

The result was a massive, blinding white ball of flame that engulfed the monster's features, causing it to shatter into thousands of icy crystal shards. This was immediately followed by the rest of the creature's body, which, with a convulsive moan, erupted into a second cascade of flames and ice.

Addie squinted through the debris to witness the last embers of her shattered foe falling to the ground.

But the shattering did not end there. The entire landscape now convulsed and heaved as a vast quake overtook it. Everything around Addie began collapsing in a torrential avalanche of fire and ice.

The rain of crystal and flame was overwhelming, its groaning, rumbling roar was deafening as all the elements collapsed around a screaming Addie, leaving only utter, silent darkness.

The first hints of dawn light over Liverpool started to illuminate the dew-soaked grounds of the Alexander house. Inside, Ezra, Rachel, and Dr. Bartlett sat nearby as Pastor Fisher read from the Psalms at Addie's bedside, "Yea, though I walk through the valley of the shadow of death, I will fear no evil…"

Suddenly, Addie's frame was racked with a violent tremor. The startled pastor looked up from his reading, "Doctor, she's…"

Dr. Bartlett came closer. The shaking only lasted a second or two. Then Addie's pale body once again lay motionless.

The doctor searched for a pulse at her wrist, then at her neck.

"Doctor, what's happening?" asked Ezra.

The doctor stood up, looking intently at Addie and stroking his beard, "Her pulse is certainly weak…"

"But she always had the heart of a lion," said Rachel in disbelief, blinking back tears and taking Addie's hand.

A voice came from the doorway: "We're here, Ezra," announced Patrick as he entered the room. Following solemnly behind him were Charlie Reynolds—removing his hat as he arrived—and Fedor, who, upon beholding the fallen Addie, halted, overcome with an unsettled sorrow, unable to take his eyes off of his broken angel. His worst fears were now realized in front of him.

Ezra rose to greet the group, shaking Charlie's hand. "Thanks so much for coming, Charlie. I know you and I had our problems, but…"

"Think nothing of it, Ezra," Reynolds said holding up his hand. "We're here to support the little lady."

"And who's this?" asked Rachel, indicating Fedor.

Ezra explained, "This is Fedor, Charlie's er…protegé. He's a performer. Patrick tells me he and Addie struck up quite a friendship backstage. I um..had some mistaken impressions."

Fedor nodded toward Rachel, "How do you do, ma'am?"

"We came as soon as I got your telegram, Ezra," began Reynolds. "I was so sorry to hear…"

"I'm afraid you're too late," declared Dr. Bartlett.

The words struck Rachel like a lightning bolt, "Oh dear God!" she sobbed as she covered her face and collapsed in Ezra's arms. Ezra himself began weeping openly. Patrick turned sadly away.

Chapter Twenty

Fedor stepped over to Addie's side to grieve, kneeling to grasp her hand, his tears spilling onto her cool, delicate skin. She had taught him much about living with physical challenges, and her indomitable spirit would be what would stay with him forever. A long moment of mournful silence filled the room.

But Addie's fingers yet showed signs of life in Fedor's hand. Startled at the unexpected movement, he stood up reflexively, "Doctor? Charlie, she's moving…"

The doctor and Ezra quickly pushed to Addie's side as Fedor stepped back. Yes, it was true; she was really stirring, her facial muscles were coming to life.

"She *is!*" exulted Ezra. "She's coming around!"

Rachel, the doctor, and the pastor all approached the bed; Fedor looked on from behind.

Addie's eyelids flickered briefly, then they opened. She

squinted and blinked for a moment, then stared unquestionably and specifically at Ezra. "Papa?"

"Addie, Sweetheart, I'm here," said Ezra as he came closer to his daughter.

"Papa I…I can *see* you!"

"What?!" cried Ezra as a stunned gasp went up from the group. Ezra looked deeply into those eyes that now returned his gaze. No longer were they the unseeing eyes he had known for twelve years but sparkling, living eyes that peered back into his own. Addie nodded at her father in affirmation. Full of astonishment, Ezra was short of breath, "Oh my!… Oh my!… It's a miracle! Oh, my dear Addie!" He embraced her, trembling. The tears of sorrow that had fallen but moments ago had transformed into those of joy and wonder.

Rachel moved closer to Addie in amazement, "How about me; can you see me?"

"Rachel!" Addie exclaimed, knowing the voice so well, "You're as beautiful as I always knew you were." She attempted to push herself up in the bed, causing Dr. Bartlett to step over to assist.

"Easy now, Miss Addie. You've had quite a bump on the head," cautioned the doctor. He then turned to Ezra. "That impact must have jarred some nerve endings or jostled a blockage. That's the only explanation I can think of."

"Or…perhaps an act of God, Doctor?" offered pastor Fisher with a smile.

Horrified that Addie would now know his true appearance, Fedor had retreated to the back of the room. Emotions were warring in his chest, his overwhelming joy that Addie could now *see*, yet, now that sight had come, knowing that his position in her life could never be the same. This agonizing conflict within him forced the conclusion that he had no choice but to withdraw; he quickly and quietly departed the room.

A beaming Addie scanned the other faces around her. "You must be Pastor Fisher," she said, pointing at the man with the parson's collar. He gently smiled and nodded. She moved on to the next face, "And you're Dr. Bartlett."

"Right again," said the doctor.

"And…Patrick?" she asked, blinking and gazing at the redhead.

"No pullin' the wool over your eyes, Kiddo," he admitted, sniffing and wiping the corner of his eye.

Addie continued until she came to Reynolds, hat in hand, looking a bit puzzled, "…and you…"

"Er…Charlie Reynolds, Dear. I uh, I brought Fedor with me…"

Addie gasped, grinning, "Where is he? May I see him?" The group looked about the room, discovering that Fedor was missing.

"Why yes…uh…he was here a moment ago," noted Reynolds.

Addie pulled herself upright in the bed, peering around, looking for Fedor. However, the weight of her injury and several motionless days in bed, combined with the flood of sensations coming into her eyes, overwhelmed her, pulling her back down. She raised her hand to her swimming head as she tried to rally her strength.

"Easy, Miss," the doctor urged as he helped support her. "Just take it slow."

"I'll try to find the boy," said Ezra, heading into the parlor. "He must be here in the house somewhere."

"I'll check the street outside," offered Charlie. The pastor joined and followed him toward the front door.

"I'll take the back yard," said Patrick as he exited.

Addie had recovered a bit and made another, stronger attempt to pull herself up, managing to sit on the edge of the bed. The doctor's hand steadied her, and Rachel came around to her other side.

"You don't have to be so brave just yet, Sweetie," cautioned Rachel. "You've been through so much."

"I have to see Fedor," Addie insisted. "It's why I came back."

Rachel and the doctor exchanged puzzled looks but Addie's plaintive tone made it clear that this was important to her. Slowly, Addie placed her feet on the floor and began to stand. She trembled slightly, closing her eyes when necessary to reduce the myriad sensations. Rachel and the doctor assisted her in coming to a full standing position.

Addie stood there for a few moments, feeling her strength begin to return. She peered around the room at what she knew must be familiar surroundings that she was now seeing for the first time. She looked at Rachel and savored her tearful smile, which brought a similar one to her own face.

"You're doing wonderfully, Sweetheart. I'm so proud of you." Rachel said as she kissed Addie's forehead.

Patrick suddenly burst back into the room. "I found him!" he told them breathlessly. "He's in the garden." Then he cautioned, "But I think he wants to be alone."

Addie scowled and, taking a tentative step, felt stronger. She then dashed toward the door, leaving the others behind before anyone could stop her.

"Addie, wait!" Rachel called after her, searching the room for a robe to give her. "You'll catch your death…"

Addie quickly scanned the house, calling out plaintively for Fedor, before heading out the back door onto the veranda. Looking out over the yard, she called for Fedor again, at last spotting him crouched and covering his face at the base of a tree near the stone garden wall.

"Fedor!" she cried, dashing down the steps and through the damp grass in her bare feet.

Fedor became frantic at her approach, "No, no, no! Stay away! Addie, please stay away! You don't want to look at me!" he wailed desperately, trembling. Addie could not quite see his face in the shadowy morning light, even if he had not raised his arms to shroud his appearance. She stopped several yards short, honoring his impassioned insistence.

Rachel and the doctor had now appeared outside, standing near the house under the pergola. Ezra and the others soon joined them. When Ezra spotted Addie and Fedor about twenty yards away and out of earshot, he began to cross the yard, but Rachel gently grabbed his arm, holding him back.

"Ezra," Rachel prompted, "Give them a moment…" Ezra looked into her eyes and nodded in agreement.

"Fedor, why do you turn away?" Addie tearfully begged. "Is it because I failed to save your kingdom? I'm so sorry…I…"

Fedor raised his eyes to heaven, crushed that she might blame herself. He knew her tears had been the beginning of what brought them to this point, and hearing the sadness in her voice again was almost more than he could bear. A sense of hopelessness burdened him—it seemed that now there was no way to keep from hurting Addie, the very thing he'd sought to avoid. He certainly could no longer maintain the ruse that he was someone other than himself. Yes, he could reveal his deception to her, further confusing and demoralizing her. Or he could run away and abandon her, hurting and confounding her gentle spirit. He could not see any positive outcomes.

A long minute of confusion and a sense of futility weighed on Fedor, and all he could do was keep himself turned away from her as he wept bitterly. Addie watched helplessly as his chest heaved in despair. Before long, though, his breathing began to calm slightly.

"Fedor?" asked Addie, sadly. He remained silent.

A realization had come to him: He had caused this heartache and knew he owed it to Addie to at last bring her the truth. Taking a deep breath, he slowly lowered his arms, gathered his resolve, and turned to face her.

Addie's expression turned to bewilderment. The voice she knew as Fedor's, but that wasn't what her eyes were telling her. "You're...you're Dog Boy?" she cried. "But...where's Fedor?"

He hesitated. "I am Fedor," he finally stated bluntly.

"What?"

"When I first saw you the day we came to the theatre, you were hurting and sad," Fedor began, "I found myself wanting to do anything, willing to go to any length to lift that sadness from you. But I didn't think such a delicate person would want to be associated with a...monster." He couldn't look her in the eye any longer. "Nor would I *want* you to be burdened by...a freak of nature."

Addie's mind was reeling, but somehow, horror was not in her.

"So I created Fedor—Charlie's assistant—so that you could believe your new friend was a normal friend, a friend who could tell you tales about life in the land of Ziymia, and I could watch your face as the sadness melted away. The stories made you happy...and that made *me* very happy," he explained.

This was a lot for Addie to absorb, and she stood stunned for several moments. Fedor had deceived her, and that hurt. But he had only done so because he believed he was protecting her. And, even then, in the deception, he had allowed her to see his inner self more clearly than any sighted person ever had. That was indeed a gift, a gift of himself.

Fedor glanced back up at her but didn't see in her face what he had expected. "You…you look on me with no fear…even now that you see me as I am?"

Addie approached and took his hands, gazing into his eyes, "I see no monster, Fedor," she told him earnestly. "I see only a kind and loving person, one of the most handsome people I've ever seen."

Fedor winced and turned away, "Come, Addie, you've only actually *seen* seven people…"

Addie couldn't help but giggle. And that, at last, brought a smile to Fedor. To be so fully accepted as a person by someone as kind and lovely and yet strong as Addie would allow him to begin to re-examine his own view of himself—and the world. Suddenly, from the spirit of one small girl, life had so many more possibilities!

"But Fedor, I've *been* to Ziymia! It's in danger! If we could just return quickly, we might still be able to save it. I promised your father I would return you to him. Your stories were all true! It's the most beautiful kingdom there ever was."

Fedor smiled gently, taking her by the shoulders and gazing into her now-living eyes, "Dearest Princess…Of *course* Ziymia is beautiful. It's a kingdom that will always exist inside you and me. You didn't fail it! It can't ever be destroyed…but with each new day faith must re-awaken it in our hearts."

"But your father, the king…" Addie pleaded, "I promised him to bring you home."

Fedor smiled, looking into her eyes. "And…you have."

Addie looked at him in wonder. Words seemed useless now,

and her heart was so full that all she could do was embrace him tenderly.

This did not escape the notice of the group standing on the lawn nearby. Ezra put his arm around Rachel as they looked on the embracing pair a few yards away.

"Well, I guess any fellow who Addie takes that kind of a shine to can't be all bad," Ezra admitted. He turned to Rachel and lowered his voice slightly. "I guess I can appreciate what it's like to feel misunderstood—and then to discover someone who truly understands you." Rachel was silent as he looked into her eyes. She smiled softly. Ezra turned back to Reynolds. "Charlie, why didn't you tell me he's so smart?"

"Gotta keep the magic and mystery alive, Ezra, my boy," said Reynolds, winking.

"Seriously though, do you think he could stay in town a few days, Charlie?" Ezra asked.

"He can stay as long as he wants as far as I'm concerned," affirmed Reynolds. When Ezra looked askance at him, Charlie drew close and whispered: "I just sold Fedor's contract to a suck…uh *fellow* named Barnum. All I have to do is get him to London by the 27th and Fedor'll be working for him while old Charlie Reynolds enjoys a nice long holiday."

"Sounds like you made out all right, Charlie," Ezra chuckled.

"Well, I don't like to brag, Ezra, my boy, but when the negotiations were over and the dust settled yours truly walked away with a sum in the high *three figures,"* Charlie boasted, placing his thumbs in his suspenders and nodding at Ezra.

Reynolds and Ezra both grinned, perhaps for different reasons. Dr. Bartlett brought Addie a blanket to try to protect her from the early morning chill. The sun had risen, however, and was now bathing the yard and gardens in a golden glow.

As the doctor warmed Addie and Fedor with the blanket, Ezra turned to Pastor Fisher. "Pastor, we've seen one miracle today; how would you like another?"

Pastor Fisher chuckled, "I'm not sure my heart could handle it, frankly. What did you have in mind?"

"How would you like to see me actually set foot inside that church of yours?" Ezra asked.

Rachel couldn't quite believe her ears, "Ezra?"

Then Ezra turned to Rachel, "But only if you'll meet me there."

Rachel's eyes widened, "Ezra, what are you saying?"

"I think it's time Addie had a real mother." Ezra took Rachel's hands. "Won't you stay, Rachel?"

Rachel looked into his eyes. His were glistening as much as hers. "Oh, Ezra!" cried Rachel. He kissed her tenderly as the rising sun transformed the morning dew into a delicate mist.

Addie, Fedor, and the Doctor had come nearer the house but hadn't heard this most recent conversation. Seeing the embrace of Rachel and Ezra came as quite a surprise: Addie and Fedor looked at each other with their own grins of wonderment.

Patrick acknowledged the couple, "Aw, I knew it all along! They were made for each other…You'd have to be *blind* not to see that!"

Addie and Fedor laughed, but to Patrick's shock, even Ezra broke forth with a hearty chuckle. Patrick gasped, "You mean I… I *did* it? Ezra, you're laughing!"

Ezra nodded, still chuckling with the others. Rachel took his arm; Addie took Fedor's, and they all headed back into the house.

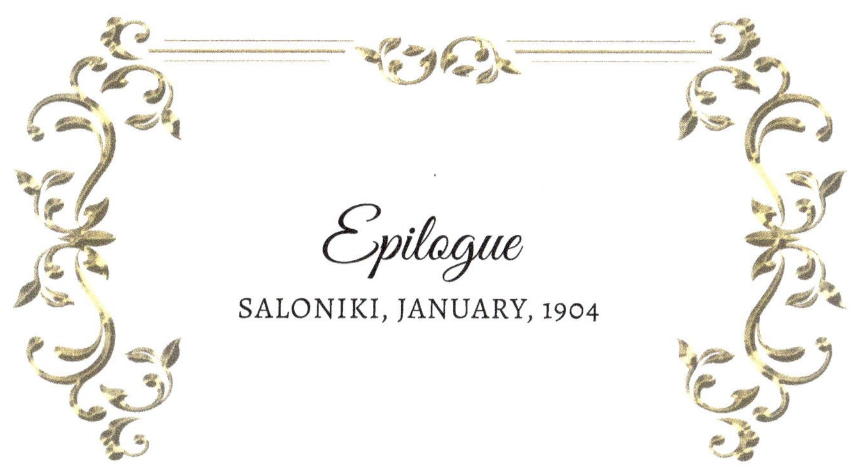

Epilogue

SALONIKI, JANUARY, 1904

Nineteen years had passed since those events in the gardens of the Alexander home, but it had scarcely been two weeks since Joseph Rutherford had interviewed Fedor. The interview had not yet been published; indeed, it was not quite complete, and Rutherford had remained in Saloniki during this time.

A horse-drawn carriage pulled up to the chalky white-arched entrance of the Sisters of Saint Theodora Hospice and Convent, built on a cliff overlooking the bay on the city's outskirts. Three travel-weary passengers disembarked—Addie, her husband Ted, and their eight-year-old son. Ted, a thin, brown-haired man of thirty-three, turned to Addie: "I'll take care of the cab. You need to hurry on in. The boy and I will be along in a minute. Off you go."

Addie smiled, gave him a quick kiss, and hastened into the convent.

The boy stayed by his father's side while Ted handed the driver some bills and instructed him as best he could to keep their luggage in the carriage and to wait for them.

It was cool inside the bleached yellow plaster building. Addie hurriedly approached one of the nuns and received some instruction accompanied by a hand gesture indicating a particular corridor. She nodded, thanked the sister, and hurried down the hallway.

Upon finding the room, from which emanated the fragrance of camphor mingled with other medicinal herbs, Addie paused briefly before entering, straightened her dress and hair, took a deep breath, and strode through the open door. Once in the room, she rounded a linen privacy screen and was presented with the sight of a prostrate and weak Fedor lying in a narrow bed. His eyes were closed, his hair matted and tangled, and a nun in a white habit sponged his forehead. It took Addie's breath away, immediately causing her throat to become tight and her eyes to well up. But she had to compose herself, at least for a few minutes…for him.

For Addie, the mere sight of Fedor caused the years to melt away. Those few days they had together in that distant summer seemed like yesterday. But then, as life moved on, she had to tend to her schooling, and Fedor went on to become a worldwide sensation under the guidance of Mr. Barnum. She revered what Fedor became and liked to believe that she had contributed to his success. But the price to be paid was that his constant travel had kept them apart. They exchanged letters, but as the years trickled past and Ted came into her life, the letters grew less frequent. And now, seeing Fedor once again, the lost connection became a regret that weighed upon Addie.

An older woman in her early fifties, wearing a dark blue full-length dress, rose from her chair and approached Addie, introducing herself in a hushed voice with a slight Russian accent, "I'm Mrs. Foerster. My husband is Fedor's manager."

"I'm Addie. Fedor and I were childhood friends. Our ship just arrived, and we got here as quickly as we could."

"He spoke of you many times, my dear. Thank you for coming," Mrs. Foerster welcomed with a calming smile.

A bearded gentleman of about forty also approached. He spoke quietly but enthusiastically, "Mrs. Lindsey! Thank you so much for coming. I'm Joseph Rutherford with the *Times of London*. Fedor has spoken so well of you. I'm very glad you came."

"As soon as I got your wire we booked passage," Addie told him, "…hoping and praying all the while that we wouldn't be too late. It was the fastest ship, but it was still a three-day journey."

Addie removed her hat and approached Fedor's bedside. She stood studying his exhausted frame, which suddenly erupted in a coughing fit that lasted most of a minute. His hands gripped the bed sheets as he struggled for air. Addie pulled up a chair and sat near him, overwhelmed with a sense of helplessness, unable to comfort Fedor.

"The doctor thinks it's pneumonia," explained Rutherford. "I was in town to interview him, but when he became ill, I decided to stay by him."

"Thank you for watching over him, Mr. Rutherford," Addie murmured.

Several minutes passed in silence as Addie watched Fedor's chest rise and fall erratically. The one whose kindness had so enduringly affected her was now a pale shadow of the lively Fedor she had known. And though she knew how deeply her husband Ted cared for her, in her heart she also knew that Ted only fell in love with the person she had become as a result of her days with Fedor.

Feeling the time was growing short, Addie rose and drew her face close to Fedor's, "Fedor...it's Addie. Can you hear me?" she said in a low tone.

Fedor's eyes slowly opened, "Addie..." he whispered. And then his lips pursed into a smile. "You're even prettier now than when we were young."

Just then, Ted and the boy appeared in the doorway. Addie motioned them over. "Fedor, this is...my husband, Ted." Then she reached out to the boy who hesitantly approached the bedside, taking his mother's hand. "And this is our son. His name is Fedor, just like you." She forced a smile.

"I'm very pleased to meet you, Fedor," said the elder Fedor, extending an unsteady hand. The wide-eyed boy took the hairy hand briefly, then retreated to his father. "Oh, now Fedor," the elder Fedor admonished weakly, "You must be brave, like your mother."

"You've become a very famous man," noted Ted to Fedor. "And, for myself, I must admit you're a bit of a difficult act to follow. We have books of clippings about you and your career and travels. Our son loves to look through them. From what Addie's told me, I feel like I've known you for a long time."

Fedor coughed again and asked, "And what do you do, Ted?"

"Both Addie and I are teachers," Ted explained. "She teaches in a school for the blind, and I teach in a Seminary."

"I teach my students to use their faith to see with their hearts, just as I learned from you," Addie told Fedor.

"I taught *you*?" Fedor asked with a wry smile. "Even then, you were the teacher. You taught me that I could be admired for myself, not how others' eyes see me. That has made me who I am. Those brief days we had together have never left me."

Fedor reached for Ted's hand, pulled him nearer, and, drawing a laboured breath, spoke in a gasping tone, "She is a treasure, Ted. Cherish her…" He was again convulsed by coughing. When it subsided, he closed his eyes, relinquished Ted's hand, and sank down in the bed, his breathing shallow.

Again, there was silence. Addie now knew exactly the sadness and dread Fedor must have felt at the side of her sickbed so long ago. Their lives were destined not to be shared, but they had each grown as a result of that precious time they'd had together.

Ted broke the silence, "Addie, the boy and I are going to wait outside for a while." Addie nodded as her family left the room.

Just then, Addie noticed something on the far bedside table. It was a lantern, identical to the beacon containing the Royal

Flame that she had carried in her sojourn in Ziymia! This one, too, burned as low as the last time she had seen it. "Fedor, the lantern. Is that yours?"

He was silent, struggling to breathe. Mrs. Foerster spoke up, "He's had that lantern as long as we've known him. He would never say exactly where it came from. But he's always kept it near him."

Addie continued looking at it in wonder. She drew closer to Fedor and whispered. "Oh, Fedor. You came to my bedside so long ago, and I was healed; you taught me to see truth with my heart…and now I really *can* see." She began to sob. "If only I could do something for you now."

Fedor's breathing had slowed and was shallower than ever. Addie drew her face near his, looked into his closed eyes, and pressed her lips to his.

With that, he breathed his last. His body, formerly tensed from the struggle to draw breath, now went limp. When it did so, unseen by Addie, a piece of cardboard he had clasped in his hand under the covers fell out onto the floor.

Rutherford and Mrs. Foerster came to the bed and put their hands on Addie as she wept loudly and uncontrollably, burying her face in the body of her dear friend.

The light in the bedside lantern had gone out.

But Rutherford noticed the item on the floor and stooped to retrieve the fallen card. In turning it over, he found that it was a miniature portrait. He raised his eyebrows, shaking his head in amazement, then shared the picture with Mrs. Foerster, who wiped her eyes and told him, "I…I've never seen that before!"

She handed it to Addie, who straightened up, dried her eyes as best she could, and took a look at the worn and faded image— it was the joyous portrait of her twelve-year-old self, standing in front of the royal palace, flanked by Brother on one side and Toybox on the other.

"One thing I do know: I was blind, and now I see." —John 9:25b

"Blessed are the pure in heart, for they shall see God." —Matthew5:8

Soli Deo Gloria

Acknowledgments

First and foremost, I must thank my wife, Mauriene, for urging me to do this story in novel form and for her patience and skills in reading, proofreading, and handholding.

I also want to acknowledge Jennifer Cronk and Pete Shrake at the Circus World Library and Research Center in Baraboo, Wisconsin, for their help.

And I wish to thank my father, whose original stories told to me and my siblings when we were children inspired both me and certain characters in this story.

Gratitude is also due to the myriad readers, advisers, and counsellors who contributed in ways large and small to help this work come to fruition.

Pikisuperstar / Freepik designed the Title Page scroll work.

—Tim Landry

Nataliia Kretsu is a Ukrainian artist with a deep passion for visual storytelling. Born October 3, 1984, she studied at the Art and Music School of the Yampil Humanitarian Lyceum in the Vinnytsia region and at the Ushynsky South Ukrainian Pedagogical University in Odesa, where she developed a strong foundation in classical art. After more than twenty years as an art teacher, she began devoting herself full-time to illustration in 2019.

Using watercolor, ink, and digital media, Nataliia blends a variety of techniques with her emotionally rich style to create illustrations that bring literary stories to life. She has collaborated with international clients on book projects, educational publications, and narrative illustration.

Nataliia's favorite projects are those that touch hearts and spark imaginations. We are privileged and honored to welcome her spirited talent in bringing the world of *Addie's Eyes* to life.

Thanks for reading!

If you've enjoyed **Addie's Eyes** and would like to encourage the creation of more books like it, would you please leave us a review? It will make a big difference.

Use this link to post on Amazon:

Amazon.com/review/create-review?&asin=B0FD95QCX7

…or scan this QR code: